JESSICA BECI
THE FINAL DONUT MYST
THE LAST DON

CW00515894

The First Time Ever Published!
The 58th and Final Donut Mystery!

Jessica Beck is the *New York Times* Bestselling Author of the Donut Mysteries, the Cast Iron Cooking Mysteries, the Classic Diner Mysteries, and the Ghost Cat Cozy Mysteries.

As always, to P and E, the very best parts of me.
And to all of you, my dear readers.
Thanks for coming along for the ride.
I couldn't have done it without you!

DONUTMAKER SUZANNE Hart's life is changing too fast for her, so when friend and bookstore owner Paige Hill offers her a weekend away, she jumps at the chance. Things aren't all they seem though, and Suzanne is again dropped into a situation where not only donuts, but murder, is on the menu. Paige's honorary aunt is having an early inheritance party to give away some of her valuable possessions before she dies, only someone at the event wants the woman's end to come sooner rather than later.

Prologue

I hadn't slept much—or frankly, all that well—for most of the night, so by midnight, when I heard a heavy thud outside my room, I was awake. Carefully turning on the flashlight on my cell phone, I glanced over at my bunkmate to see if they'd heard the noise too.

The only problem was that the other bed was empty.

Had that been her falling outside? I'd had a very long day, but I suddenly got a burst of adrenaline as I got up and rushed to the door.

"Paige, is that you? Are you okay?" I asked as I threw the door open to check on what had happened.

There was indeed a body lying in the hallway, the face eerily illuminated by the light of my phone, but it wasn't who I'd been expecting.

I flipped on the hall light to see who had fallen.

It hadn't been an accident.

There was no doubt about that.

It was someone else I recognized, though, and from the depth the letter opener had been plunged into the victim's chest, I knew that there was very little I could do to save them.

As I leaned over the body and searched for a pulse in vain, someone joined me without me knowing it.

"Why did you do it, Suzanne?" a voice asked me, and as I looked up at my accuser, I realized that to the unsuspecting eye, it appeared that I had indeed been the one who had committed this murder and not the person who had just discovered it.

I had been in some tight places before, but never one as tight as this one appeared to be, and it was most likely going to take everything I had to dig myself out of it.

Chapter 1

"Suzanne, I'm leaving," my best friend, Grace Gauge, said as she walked into my donut shop one chilly winter day. The thermometer registered a few notches below freezing, but with the winds gusting outside, it felt more like single digits to me.

That was more than a little too cold for my part of North Carolina, at least as far as I was concerned. I'd been feeling a bit under the weather for the last few days, probably from something I'd eaten, and I'd skipped breakfast that morning. Even the smell of donuts, an aroma I had once adored above all others, made me feel a bit unsettled.

"How can you leave? You just got here," I asked Grace with a smile as I poured her a cup of coffee and handed it over without being asked. This was the one day of the week when I worked the shop solo, so honestly, I was glad for the company.

Grace took it gratefully, had a large sip, and then explained, "I'm sorry. I didn't know how to break it to you, so I thought I'd just blurt it out. My company is being bought out by one of the giants in the cosmetics industry. I'm under a strict nondisclosure order, so all I can say is that it's happening, and very soon."

"A gag order from the top hasn't stopped you before," I told her as I added a donut hole flavor I was trying out to a plate and handed it to her. It was my new take on hot cocoa with peppermint and a hint of cinnamon, but I wasn't sure if I'd gotten it right yet. "What do you think?"

"This one has real teeth. I'd better not violate it," Grace said as she took a bite. She glanced around the dining area, though we were alone, at least for the moment. That was another reason I hated the weather. My customers tended to stay in where it was warm and cozy, not that I could blame them. I was thinking more and more lately that it wouldn't be a bad idea at all, staying home and letting the world go on at its own pace without me. I hadn't been feeling like my old self the past few weeks, run-down and a bit crankier than normal, and staying in bed sounded pretty good to me. But running the donut shop was my responsibility, at least on the days I was in charge. My assistant, Emma Blake, and her mother, Sharon, took over two days a week for me, but I was beginning to wish it were more.

I'd learned that even the joy of donutmaking can get old if you've done it a few thousand times.

"The donut has teeth?" I asked her as she took another nibble.

"No, the nondisclose," Grace answered as she took another small bite of the morsel I'd offered. "This has a bit *too* much flavor for my taste," she said as she pushed the donut hole remnant aside. "But don't trust my judgment. I've been feeling a bit off lately, and nothing really tastes all that good to me. How are you?"

"Not great," I admitted.

"Suzanne, I think we must have gotten some bad burritos from that new food truck the other day. I knew stopping at Maple Hollow for lunch wasn't a good idea."

"Probably not, but let's get back to the donut. What is it? Is there too much cocoa? Cinnamon? Or peppermint?" I asked.

"Yes," she said. "To all of the above."

"I'll keep working on it," I told her as I threw the leftover piece away. That was the way it went sometimes with new recipes. It was a rare treat that I got right the first time. "Now, where are you going, and when will you be back?"

Grace looked as though she was about to cry, something that was extremely unusual for my best friend. This was clearly something different from all those times before. "Grace, what is it?"

"That's what I've been trying to tell you. I'm leaving April Springs," she said, clearly upset by the prospect.

Not as much as I was, though.

"Do you *have* to go?" I asked her. "They've tried to make you take promotions before, but you've always managed to get out of them in the past."

"I'm not sure that I *want* to turn this one down," she admitted. "I'll be running an entire division out of San Francisco. You know me. I've *always* dreamed of living there."

"What about your husband?" I asked her. Stephen Grant was our local chief of police, and I couldn't imagine him giving up his job as our law enforcement head to follow her across the country.

"It's a package deal. He's going to be head of security for my division. They knew how to get to me, Suzanne. This place does their homework."

"And Stephen's okay with it?" I asked incredulously.

"You know as well as I do that the job has taken a toll on him ever since he took over as chief, *and* it hasn't been all that good for our marriage. He wants a fresh start, and he told me last night that all he cares about is being with me. I know I'll miss April Springs, but the truth is, I'm going to miss you most of all."

I came around the counter and hugged her. I was still in a state of shock. Grace had flirted with leaving town a few times in the past, but this was clearly much more serious.

"Should I try to get out of it so I can stay here with you?" she whispered as she choked back her tears. "I don't want to lose you in my life, Suzanne. We're sisters by every definition but biological."

"Hey, you can't pass up on your dream job in a city you've idealized since we were kids," I told her, stunned that I was trying to convince my best friend to leave. "You have to do it, Grace."

"I know deep down that you're right," she admitted. "Will you at least promise to come visit me?"

"Of course I will. Jake and I have been talking about taking more vacations. I can see accumulating some massive frequent flier miles in my future," I said with a grin, fighting the tears myself.

"Okay. I can come back here too. I really do want to tackle this. In my world, it's the big time."

"You're going to knock them dead, kiddo," I told her.

"Thanks for that," she said.

"Besides, I'm sure we've got months and months to get used to the idea before you have to go," I reassured her. Something in her expression told me that I was wrong. "Weeks?" No response, so I asked, "Days?"

"Hours," she admitted reluctantly. "The company is packing things up for us, and we've got an apartment there for six months until we find a place of our own."

"Wow, this is really happening fast, isn't it?" I asked her. A thought suddenly occurred to me. "Is Stephen going with you today, or is he joining you later?"

"We're both booked out of Charlotte Douglas Airport on the red-eye tonight. Stephen is giving the mayor his letter of resignation even as we speak," she admitted.

"But that's going to leave the chief of police job open," I reasoned. "Are any of Stephen's deputies ready to take over?"

"I'm not sure how to answer that," Grace said cagily.

"Why, because you don't know, or you can't say? Don't tell me your husband made you sign a nondisclose too."

"No, but it's not my place to tell you," she said as I saw our mayor, George Morris, approaching the donut shop, with Stephen Grant just behind him. I ignored them for the moment, though, because of the third man in the party.

It was my husband, former state police investigator and onetime April Springs Chief of Police Jake Bishop, and I had a cold chill sweep through me.

I *knew* why they were all coming to Donut Hearts, and it wasn't for one of my treats.

I had a feeling I was about to get the second bad piece of news that morning, and I wasn't looking forward to hearing it any more than I was to learn that Grace was leaving town for good.

"It's just temporary, Suzanne," Jake explained for the third time after everyone else had gone. I didn't blame them. I wouldn't have stuck around either if I could have helped it.

"Jake, it's too dangerous. You retired from active police work, remember?"

"Suzanne, we're not talking about Charlotte or Raleigh. This is April Springs. Besides, you heard the mayor. It's not forever. There will be a new chief in a month or two, and I'll be off the hook. I couldn't say no. They need me."

"So do I," I told him.

He wrapped me up in his arms and hugged me fiercely. Normally, I loved being in my husband's embrace, but not so much this time. "I don't like it," I said with a muffled voice.

Jake pulled away. "If you want me to go back to the mayor and tell him I can't do it, then that's what I'll do. I don't want to, but I'll do it if it's that important to you."

I knew that he would, too, but I couldn't be the reason he broke a promise. "No, it's the right thing to do. Just make *me* one promise, will you?"

"I'll do it if I can," he said.

"Once they find a replacement, don't ever get into this situation again, no matter how much they say they need you. I need you, too, and that should take precedence over the town."

"I promise," he said.

"I mean it, Jake."

"So do I," he said. Changing gears, he asked softly, "How are you holding up? I'm so sorry Grace is leaving."

"Honestly, I'm still in shock. It's going to take some time for it to even sink in."

He put a hand on my shoulder. "It'll be okay, Suzanne."

"I doubt it, but thanks for saying so."

Jake nodded. We'd been married long enough that he knew when to push and when to back off, and this was definitely one of those "back off" moments. "Well, I'd better get over to the station. If you need me, you know where to find me."

"Be careful," I told him, more out of habit than anything else.

"Crossing the street?" he asked me with a grin, since the station was less than a hundred yards away from my shop.

"It's more of a general suggestion than a specific instruction," I told him.

I gave him credit for not laughing. "I promise."

My mother came in ten minutes after Jake left.

"You're not usually a morning donut person, Momma. You've already heard the news, haven't you?"

My diminutive mother scoffed. "Suzanne Hart, can't a mother visit her daughter without having an ulterior motive?"

"Sure she can, but she usually doesn't," I told her with a grin.

"I *may* have heard something in the wind this morning," Momma reluctantly admitted.

"Which part do you know about?"

"Both of them, unless something else has happened besides Grace and Stephen leaving town and Jake taking over as the chief of police."

"*Temporary* chief of police," I corrected her. "Word gets around fast here, doesn't it?"

"You know this town as well as I do. Gossip is an Olympic sport in April Springs. How are you dealing with it all?"

"I'll admit that at first, I was devastated, but then I decided to be a grown-up and be happy for Grace," I said, and then I quickly added, "I lied. I'm still mostly just devastated."

"What did I teach you as a child, Suzanne?"

"Never stick a fork in an electrical outlet?" I asked innocently.

"Suzanne," she prodded.

"Life is all about change," I repeated. "You have to learn to roll with the punches, or you'll never get back up again when it knocks you down. I still think it was a little harsh teaching that to a preschooler."

"I disagree," she said. "Now, what can I do to help?"

"Buy out my stock so I can go home and mope," I told her with a shrug as I gestured to the donuts behind me, just joking.

"I can do that," she said, whipping out her checkbook. "How much for everything in the cases?"

"Momma, I was just teasing."

"I wasn't," she said. "I'm deadly serious. I've been meaning to make a donut donation to a shelter in Charlotte. This is the perfect time."

"Momma," I chided her.

"Suzanne," she replied in the same tone of voice.

Ordinarily, I would have fought her on it, but at the moment, I didn't have any fight left in me. "Fine." I quoted her a figure after looking around the shop that would have made anyone else flinch, but she didn't bat an eye.

"Is that retail, or am I getting the family discount?" she asked archly.

"That's full retail," I told her, hedging the truth a little. "Mostly."

"I don't think you charge enough. I'm adding a twenty-five percent surcharge for the short notice," Momma said as she wrote out the check. She was one of the few people I knew who still bothered carrying her checkbook around with her.

I knew better than to argue with her. "Fine. I'll box them up, but I can't deliver them."

"No worries. I'll have Geneva take care of it."

Geneva Swift was Momma's assistant. We'd had a rocky start, but we'd become friendly, if not friends, lately.

"Sounds good. Thanks, Momma."

"Of course. It's the least I can do."

"No, the least you can do is pat me on the back and tell me to put on my big-girl pants, that life isn't fair, and that I need to get over it." These were all things she'd said to me in the past, and some of them not so long ago.

"Well, those apply, too, but you don't need chiding at the moment."

"That's certainly true enough, Momma. I love you."

"I love you too, Daughter Dearest," my mother said.

Twenty minutes after she left, I was just boxing up the last of the donuts when Geneva arrived with three movers and a panel truck. "I hear you have some donuts for us, ma'am," Geneva said with a smile.

"As a matter of fact, I've got *all* of them," I answered as I handed her a coffee. "How about you gentlemen? Would you care for hot beverages and a treat?"

It was clear that two of them wanted to say yes, but the man who was evidently in charge shook his head. "Thanks, but no thanks. We have work to do. Gentlemen, let's get busy."

As they worked, I filled three cups anyway, since I was just going to have to throw it out once they were gone. I wasn't about to stay open to sell the last of my coffee.

They loaded the treats in short order while Geneva and I chatted, and as they were leaving, I handed the tray with the coffees to the leader. "I insist."

He wanted to say no, but I could tell that he'd have a full-blown mutiny on his hands if he did, so he gracefully accepted.

I cleaned up the shop, and at ten minutes after ten, well before my usual closing time, I locked Donut Hearts up.

I was done for the day.

The next question was, now what?

Chapter 2

I'd promised myself I would let Grace pack in peace, but I couldn't help myself. I pulled my Jeep in behind her company car and walked up to her front door. She must have heard me coming, because she met me there before I could ring the bell.

"What took you so long?" she asked, crying as she hugged me.

"I got here as soon as I could. Would it be selfish of me to ask you not to take this big promotion and live in a city you've always loved after all?"

"I would be crushed if you didn't at least *try* to get me to stay," she replied as we walked inside together.

"Where's your husband?" I asked as I looked around.

"He's taking care of some last-minute business, going over some things with yours. He asked me to pack a bag for him, and I'm tempted to put in all of his heaviest winter clothes."

"Is it as cold there as it is here?"

"No," she said with a grin. "But it's still pretty chilly. I'm just teasing. He's doing something huge for me, and I'm not about to sabotage it."

"I still can't believe you're leaving me," I said.

"I can't, either. There's always FaceTime and Skype and other ways for us to keep in touch. I'm so sorry." Grace clearly looked upset about her decision, and I realized that I really was being selfish. It was time for me to act like a grown-up and not some spoiled little kid. I wiped my tears away and did my best to smile. "Enough of this gloom and doom. We'll be out to visit as soon as you get settled, so I hope this place they've set you up in has an extra bedroom."

"Three of them, actually," she admitted.

"Wow, you really are a big shot now, aren't you?"

"I'm living in fear that they'll realize they made a mistake promoting me and take it all back."

"Nonsense," I said as I touched her arm lightly. "You're going to be great. I just know it."

"That makes one of us," she said. Grace got more serious as she said, "Suzanne, with me leaving town, maybe it's time you retired as an amateur sleuth."

"Hey, I've solved more than a few cases without you, though it's been the most fun working with you over the years."

"That's not what I mean. I'm afraid one of these days, a close call is going to be too close, and I'll never see you again. At least promise me you'll think about hanging it up for good."

"I have, believe me, but I keep getting dragged into things," I told her.

"We both know you can't get dragged anywhere you don't want to be," Grace said with a smile.

"To be fair, that sounds more like you than me," I countered.

"Touché," she replied. "I just can't bear the thought of something happening to you when I'm clear across the country."

"I'll give it some thought. Honestly, I've been playing with the idea myself for quite a while. I'm getting a little too old to face down killers." It was true too. There had been a few times in the past where my investigations had put my life in jeopardy, and I didn't like admitting that I'd been good, but I'd also been lucky, and everyone knows that at some point in everyone's life, the luck simply runs out.

"That's all I can ask," she said.

I looked around her place. "Is there anything I can do to help you?"

"No, I'm afraid I need to do this alone. Will you look after the place while I'm gone? I can't bring myself to sell it, at least not yet."

I couldn't imagine anyone else living in Grace's home, but of course she'd sell it. I'd been living in a fantasy world thinking that things would always stay the same. "You bet." I felt myself tearing up again, so I knew I had to get out of there before I started bawling again. "If you're sure you don't need me, I'll take off."

"I will always need you, and you know it," Grace said as she hugged me again, this time more fiercely than she had before.

"Right back at you," I told her.

I held my tears until I pulled away, but I was just starting to cry again when I noticed someone sitting on my front porch swing in front of the cottage I shared with Jake.

Wiping my reddened cheeks, I did my best to smile as I greeted my friend, Paige Hill. What brought her to my place when her bookstore, The Last Page, was still open?

"Suzanne, are you okay?" she asked, her voice full of empathy. "I just heard Grace was leaving town, so I went by Donut Hearts to see you, but you were already gone. I am so sorry."

"It's okay," I said, stifling a sniffle.

"Hey, I'm your friend too. You can talk to me. You know that, right?"

"Fine. You want the truth? I'm miserable," I admitted with a shrug, "but there's nothing I can do about it."

"That stinks," she said.

After a moment, I asked her with a smile, "That's it? That's all you've got for me? That it stinks?"

"Hey, I never claimed to have a cure. I just figured it might help to have some company."

"It does, but what about the bookstore?"

"My assistant is more than capable of running The Last Page, as long as there are no important decisions she has to make."

I laughed. "Is she that bad?"

Paige waved a hand in the air. "She is, but it doesn't matter. I didn't come over to discuss my employee issues," she said. "I came over to help you get through this."

I took a deep breath and then let it out slowly. "I'm going to be all right. It's just going to take a little time. Is that really the *only* reason you came by?"

"Well, there *was* one thing I was going to ask you about, but that was before I found out about Grace." The elfin blonde looked at her hands, and I wondered what was on her mind.

"Humor me. I could use the distraction," I told her.

"Fine, but it's okay if you want to say no. I got an invitation to my aunt Jenny's Early Inheritance party in Porter Mountain, and I'd love you to be my plus-one."

"I never heard you mention an aunt. And what on earth is an Early Inheritance party?" I asked her.

"First off, she's not *really* my aunt. She and my mom were roommates in college, so it's an honorary thing. Jenny married her childhood sweetheart, who then surprised everyone by inventing some kind of doohickey that cut a step out of fabricating something used in computers or something. I don't know, the details are beyond me, but he made a boatload of money, and they got really rich.

"Anyway, he died a few years ago, and Jenny was lost. We were all worried about her. She became obsessed with dying, so to combat it, she started throwing these parties once a year to give away something of hers while she's alive so she can enjoy giving the gift. It's a three-day soiree at her mansion in the mountains. The place is truly spectacular. Don't worry about intruding. You don't have to be family to come; *none* of us are. She never had kids, and her real family died off long ago, so she invites a gaggle of odds and ends who have ties to her instead."

"I wouldn't want to impose," I told her. "The truth is, I probably wouldn't be a very good houseguest." The party sounded a little crazy to me, but I could see some merit in the woman's desire to give away some of her things so she could enjoy it, as opposed to it all happening after she was gone.

"Are you kidding? She'd *love* to meet you. I've told her all about you, so you might have to make a few donuts for her while you're there, since she adores them. Besides, some of the people who will be there are absolute jackals, at least as far as I'm concerned. They can't wait for her to die so they can get their hands on a piece of her fortune. I go mostly to protect her from the pack, but I can use someone there who has my back. What do you say? I know it's asking a lot, and if you say no, I'll totally understand, but it would mean the world to me. Suzanne, the change of scenery might even do you some good."

I wanted to say no, I really did, but Paige was a good friend of mine, and she needed my help. I always had a hard time saying no to my friends. As faults go, there were a great many worse ones I could have had, at least as far as I was concerned. "I'll go, on two conditions."

"Shoot," she said.

"Emma and Sharon have to be okay with running the donut shop while I'm gone, and Jake has to be okay with it."

"Done and done," she said.

"Oh, and one more thing."

"I'm listening," she said.

"I don't want to leave town until Grace is gone. She's leaving this evening."

"I understand, but we need to be there in time for dinner when everything kicks off," Paige said. "When exactly does Grace leave?"

"I don't know. Let's go find out," I said.

My last condition turned out not to be a factor in my decision at all.

When we got to Grace's place, she was already gone.

I'd just lost my best friend for what felt like forever.

Maybe Paige was right.

Maybe getting away was exactly what I needed.

"Fine. Let me go home and make a few calls. I'll let you know as soon as I find out if I'm free."

"Sounds great! Thanks, Suzanne."

"I'm not sure I can even go, so don't thank me too soon," I said.

"Hey, you're trying. That's good enough for me."

Jake was my first call. After I explained the situation to him, he was all for me going. "Not that I won't miss you, but honestly, the job's going to need my full attention for the next few weeks anyway, so I won't be much company for you at home."

"Is the department really in that bad a shape?" I asked, wondering if Stephen Grant had made a mess of the April Springs Police Department during his time as chief.

"It's been sufficient for him, but it's not the way I do things. Let's just say that some of his methods are a bit unconventional. I want to bring things back in line so the next guy can step in without missing a beat. Don't worry about me. I'll be fine. Does going to this party sound like fun to you?"

I thought about that for a second. Fun? Nothing sounded like fun at the moment. But would it do me good to get away? I didn't see what harm it could do. "Sure. It'll be good."

"Come on, enjoy the adventure. I expect reports back from the lap of luxury, though, okay?"

"Paige said I'd probably be making donuts while I'm there. Evidently her aunt loves them."

"So much the better. It will give you something to do. I love you, Suzanne."

"I love you too. Let me call Emma and Sharon, and if they're good with it, I'll go. I'm sure they'll be fine, though. Should I stop off and say good-bye on my way out of town?"

"You can try, but I have no idea where I'll be," he said. "I want to do some checks on the troops while they are in the field."

"You don't miss a beat, do you?" I asked. My husband was thorough and competent and the most able law enforcement officer there ever was, at least as far as I was concerned.

"I try not to," he said. "Safe travels."

"Thanks," I said.

"Emma, would you and your mother mind running Donut Hearts for the next three days? Paige needs me out of town for something." I didn't feel the need to go into any more detail than that.

"Yes," she said simply.

"You'd mind? Really?" That was unexpected.

"What? No, I meant yes, we'd be glad to do it. Suzanne, I need to talk to you about something, and it can't wait. When are you leaving?"

"As soon as I can pack," I admitted. "You're quitting, aren't you?" I'd been afraid of that very thing for years. After all, I knew she was cut out for better and brighter things than helping me run a donut shop.

"No. Of course not. Just the opposite, in fact."

"What's the opposite of quitting?" I asked her.

"Mom and I will be there in five minutes. Don't go anywhere, please."

"I'll need at least ten to get my things together," I told her. "What's this about, Emma?"

"Talk soon," she said, dodging my question.

I was zipping up my garment bag with my two best, basically my *only* two, nice dresses when the doorbell rang.

"Right on time," I said as I let the mother and daughter in. "Come on back to my bedroom. We can talk there."

As I started stowing things in my suitcase, a neat hard-shelled carry-on bag that had wheels and a telescoping handle, they started talking.

"Since the Barton fiasco, Mom and I still need to invest our inheritance in a restaurant, and we want to make another pitch to you."

"We really want to buy Donut Hearts," Sharon interjected.

"Don't say no. Hear us out first," Emma said quickly.

"I'll listen to what you have to say," I told them. I stopped packing and sat on the bed. "You've got my full and undivided attention."

"Suzanne, we need this," Emma told me. "Donut Hearts is in our blood, and since we've been running things more and more over the years, we've come to realize that we want to work there together."

Sharon smiled gently at her daughter and nodded. "We're willing to pay you over the fair market value." She handed me an offer sheet that was for quite a bit more than I thought Donut Hearts was worth, and that was saying something. With that kind of money, I could take my time to figure out what came next in my life.

As I folded the paper and tucked it into my back jeans pocket, Emma took a deep breath and then continued. "Tell the truth. You've got to be getting tired of making donuts all of the time. I've seen it in your eyes lately. You need a major change in your life, and this will allow you to try something new."

"I *love* making donuts," I said, more as an automatic protest than a true expression of feeling. I was getting tired of the routine of getting up in the middle of the night and going to bed when most folks were just sitting down to dinner.

"I know that," Emma said hastily.

"*We* know that," Sharon added. "If we're out of line, we apologize, but we had to ask. Tell you what. Why don't you take a few days and think about it. Clearly, you're going away," she said as she gestured to my packing. "Otherwise, you wouldn't need us to step in. Not that we mind. Donut Hearts has become our home as well."

"Play around with the idea for a few days before you answer us, that's all we ask," Emma said. "Enjoy living life during regular hours for a change of pace. With Jake being retired, you two could travel or even find a business you could run together."

"Jake's not retired," I said flatly.

"He went back to work?" Emma asked. "Oh, no. I'm so sorry."

"It's just temporary," I told them, "until they can find a replacement for Stephen Grant."

"Chief Grant is quitting? Why?" Emma asked.

Clearly, not everyone had heard the news about Grace and Stephen. It struck me as a bit ironic that the newspaper publisher's own family didn't know the biggest development in April Springs in months. "Grace is leaving...in fact, she's already left for a new job in San Francisco, and Stephen went with her."

"That's terrible," Emma said as she hugged me. "Forget what we said. We didn't know."

"Hang on," Sharon added. "Maybe you should keep our offer in mind after all. It's going to take a month or two for them to find a replacement for the chief. You can stay on until they do, and when Jake steps down, you can too."

"I'll give it some serious thought," I said, "but right now, I really have to finish packing. I need to pick Paige up on our way out of town."

"It could be great for..." Emma was interrupted by her mother's gentle grip on her shoulder.

"She said she'd think about it. Now, let's get out of her hair."

Emma finally understood. She and Sharon headed for the door without another word, and I was left to pack the last few things I thought I'd need.

As I finished up, I considered their offer.

I couldn't sell Donut Hearts. I'd built it into a thriving—well, maybe not thriving, but a sound business nonetheless. That wasn't something I could just walk away from.

Or could I? Emma was right. I had begun to grow tired of the daily grind of early rising, donutmaking, and early bedtime. But could I just walk away from everything, no matter how generous their offer was?

Maybe, just maybe, I could.

But I didn't have to make up my mind that second. Zipping the suitcase up, I grabbed it and my garment bag and headed for my Jeep.

Everything had come at me too fast today, and getting away, at least temporarily, sounded like a solid plan.

At least it seemed like it at the time.

Chapter 3

After we got out of April Springs and headed toward the mountains, I asked Paige, "Could you tell me something about your aunt Jenny?"

"Let's see. She's in her early sixties, which I used to think was ancient, but the older I get, the younger it seems. I've always been impressed with how graceful she is. Oh, and she has the most beautiful chestnut hair I've ever seen in my life."

"What's she like, though?"

"There are two Aunt Jennys in my mind, the one before her husband died and the one after. She shows glimpses of who she used to be now and then, but he was the love of her life, and without him, she's faded some. She lights up when I tell her stories about you, though."

"About me?" I asked, puzzled to hear it. "She must really love donuts."

"Actually, it's your hobby she's more interested in than your profession," Paige admitted.

"Crime solving?" I asked.

"Aunt Jenny *loves* to hear the tales of your exploits." Paige paused and then stared at me. "I hope you don't mind me telling her about your adventures."

"Adventures? Is that what you call them? Bouts of dangerous insanity is what I call them."

"Come on, you've managed to come out on top every time."

"So far, at least. Let's get back to your honorary aunt."

Paige bit her lower lip for a second and then said, "The sparks of the old Aunt Jenny are coming less and less as the years pass by. I wonder if I'll ever find the kind of love she had for Uncle Gray."

"It took me quite a while to find mine, and it even took more than once," I told her.

"Yeah, but when you got it right, you really got it right."

"How about the other guests?" I asked as I approached the first incline leading us up to our destination. Rain mixed with sleet, and I wondered if it might be snowing at the higher elevation we were going to. My Jeep had all-weather tires, so we should be fine, but I was glad that I was the one driving.

"Let's see. Unless I miss my guess, there will be four other guests and two employees there with us this weekend."

"How big a house does she own that she needs people there waiting on her?" I asked. "You said it was nice, but come on."

"It's pretty swanky. Roberta is her maid/personal assistant and any other job that needs doing inside except cooking. She's very efficient, though not all that emotional, at least as far as I can tell. Nothing seems to faze her."

"Who does the cooking?" I asked, naturally curious, given my line of work.

"That would be Calvin. He's quite the chef, and the handyman as well. He's worked for Aunt Jenny for years, and sometimes I think maybe he's a little *too* familiar with her, if you know what I mean."

I took a chance and glanced over at Paige. "Do you mean they are...involved?"

"Ew. Not like that. I just meant he's a little too brash with her at times. There's nothing else going on there. Trust me."

"You don't sound as though you like this Calvin very much," I said.

"Does it really show? No, I'm not a fan, but she likes him fine, so I'm staying out of it."

"You're butting out of other people's lives? I wouldn't know what that's like," I replied with a grin. "I don't seem to have mastered that art myself. Otherwise, I wouldn't find myself constantly getting involved with murder and mayhem."

"Do you mean it's not all by choice?" Paige asked me.

"Hardly. It usually starts with me helping out a friend or being dragged into something against my will. If it were up to me, I'd never deal with another murder again as long as I live."

Paige nodded. "I get that. I've read about crime so much at the bookstore that I'm almost desensitized to it, but that's all on paper and *never* face to face. I don't know how you do it."

"If I have any say in the matter, I won't ever be doing it again."

"But like you said, it hasn't really been your choice most of the time in the past," Paige observed.

It was time to get back to the subject at hand. Besides, I didn't really want to talk about my motivation for finding killers. "How about the other guests?"

"Of course. Let's see, as far as I know, it will be Bess Wilkshire, Sandy Erickson, Frank Palmer, and Bobbi Nash staying the weekend. Aunt Jenny might have added others to the list, but that's all I know about."

"You never know. After all, I was a last-minute addition myself." A thought suddenly occurred to me. "Paige, I don't care either way, but was my coming with you *your* idea or your aunt's?"

My friend shook her head. "Wow, you really *are* good at deducing things, aren't you?"

"So it was your Aunt Jenny's idea?"

"She mentioned last night that she'd love to meet you, so I thought I'd invite you to join me on the trip. Suzanne, I hope you don't mind. I'm thrilled she suggested you come. We don't get to spend that much time together."

"With Grace gone, I'm going to have more free time than I know what to do with, so that might change." I realized how that must have sounded. "Wow, what a terrible thing to say. You're not my second choice, Paige. I've just known Grace practically since we were toddlers."

"Hey, I get it. It's the whole silver and gold thing from the kids' song," she said.

I started singing, "Make new friends but keep the old," and she joined in. We laughed simultaneously. "Girl scout?" she asked.

"You betcha. You too?"

Oh, yes."

A few minutes later, I said, "Tell me about the folks I'll be meeting."

"Let's see. Bess is in her late twenties. She's a pretty stunning redhead with an hourglass figure, and she uses all of it to her full advantage. Don't make the mistake of thinking that she's ditzy, though. There's a streak of smart and cunning that she hides really well, and she's made a life exploiting the fact that most people underestimate her."

"How did she happen to get to be in your aunt's inner circle?" I asked as I dodged a downed tree branch in the road.

"I have no idea. I'm not sure why any of them are in her closest group."

"Okay. Who else is there?"

"Sandy. She seems shy, but there's something always in her eyes that tells me more is going on than it appears. I have a hunch those still waters run very deep. Then there's Frank Palmer. He's a model of the ideal-looking man, handsome, rakish, and a really smooth operator."

"Why is he a model?" I asked. "Is he really that handsome?"

"No, I mean yes, but I was talking more about his size. Frank is five foot four in his boots, and he's let his bantam size drive him his entire life, from what I've gathered. He hates being teased about his size, and he has a temper that is quick to flare up at the slightest provocation."

"Got it," I said, making a note to myself to tread carefully with him. Not that I would have commented on his size, but I wanted to guard myself against saying anything that could be construed as an insult about his height, or more specifically, his lack thereof.

"That leaves Bobbi," she said with a sigh. "She's been through some things, though I don't know what they might have been. Bobbi is in her late forties, but she looks older than Aunt Jenny. Oh, and she has one droopy eyelid, so she wears her hair over it, like Veronica Lake used to. Do you know who she was?"

"The femme fatale from the 1940s with the peekaboo hairstyle? Oh, yes," I said.

"Well, don't expect the glamour or beauty, just the coif," Paige told me.

"Wow, that sounds like quite the collection of people," I told her as the road became narrower and narrower. "I'd better concentrate on getting us there safely. This road's getting a little dicey," I said as the rain started freezing on the road.

"We're nearly there. Just one more bridge and then we'll be at her house," Paige explained.

I slowed down and made my way carefully across the bridge in question, trying not to look down over the side to see just how high up we were. I saw a cell phone tower nearby, so at least we should have service. I must have been holding my breath, because once we were across and pulling into the parking area a thousand more feet down the narrow drive, I finally allowed myself to exhale.

"That was kind of hairy, wasn't it?" Paige asked. "It's supposed to warm up in a few days, so we should be fine heading home. In the meantime, let's get inside and meet the gang."

"After you," I said as I got out and grabbed my luggage.

I wasn't sure what the next three days might bring, but at least it might serve to take my mind off Grace's departure, and if it could do that, even for a little bit, then the trip would be worth it.

The house was, as promised, truly spectacular. It offered the best features of midcentury modern, built with clean lines, low and long.

The building appeared to have grown naturally from its surroundings, evolving in place instead of being built. The front of the home featured yards and yards of glass, wooden beams, and stone. The shape of the house was asymmetrical, and that helped disguise just how large it really was. As Paige and I carried our bags up onto the front porch, I took in the massive portico of slate laid in dark concrete. And then I took in the expansive size of the wooden door. It appeared to be made of solid mahogany, patterned with book-matched chevrons of differing tones and hues but all clearly made of the same species of wood. The door handles and hinges, epic pieces of wrought iron, were dark and dimpled, as though they had been hammered on a forge a hundred years earlier.

In short, the place was magnificent, and it took my breath away. How could someone own a home like this? Even the landscaping around it was lush. I saw a pond nearby and gardens that were stark this time of year but promised the hint of beauty once the weather warmed. The entire property was beyond my realm of comprehension. I usually didn't envy people things they possessed, but I wanted that house and the grounds. It was love at first sight, but one that was bound to go unrequited. If I took every dime I had, I knew that I still couldn't afford the annual tax payments on the place, let alone the upkeep and mortgage installments I would face every month.

Still, a girl could dream, couldn't she?

Paige took in my rapt expression. I hadn't even noticed her until I glanced over and saw her grinning at me. "It's something, isn't it?"

"You didn't do it justice," I said, rubbing the smooth, polished wood.

"Suzanne, you've got to admit that it's kind of tough to describe," she answered.

"That's true enough. It should be some kind of museum, not a private home." I realized how that must have sounded. "I didn't mean it that way. I'm sure your Aunt Jenny enjoys every second living here."

Paige's grin faded slightly. "Not so much lately, but yeah, she knows how lucky she is." After a moment, my friend asked me with a grin, "So, are you ready to face the jackals?"

"I'm not so sure about that, but I'd love to meet your aunt Jenny."

"Then you're in luck. She told me this morning when I let her know that I was able to convince you to come that we should go straight to the study and bypass everyone else. She wants a private audience with you first."

"Not you too?" I asked, wondering what that meant.

Paige frowned. "I'm not sure. We'll have to ask her. Come on. It'll be fine. You're going to love her. I just know it."

"I hope so," I said as Paige opened the massive door.

I thought it would take some effort to move something so large and substantial, but she'd made it look like child's play. Paige saw my frown and answered before I could ask the question. "It's perfectly balanced to open at a mere whisper. The house really is amazing."

"I don't have any trouble believing that," I said as we walked in to be greeted by a nice, weathered-looking man in his midforties. He had an apron on, and I could see that his hands had been well used in the course of his life. This had to be Calvin.

He nodded. "Ladies. If you'll let me take your bags, Jen is waiting in the study."

Paige looked a little surprised by the familiar way he said her aunt's name. "Stooping to being a doorman now, Calvin? Isn't that beneath you?" She asked it with a slight smile, but I could feel the tension between them.

"I'm doing it as a favor to your *aunt*," he said. The way he emphasized the last word made it obvious that he didn't approve of the implication that he was a mere servant.

"Aren't you sweet," Paige said as she offered her bags.

"I can carry my own, thanks anyway," I told him with a smile that was a bit warmer than Paige's had been. "I'm Suzanne, by the way, and you must be Calvin. I've heard great things about your cooking. I can't wait."

He shrugged as he plucked my bags from me anyway. "I do what I can."

Without another word, he pivoted and walked down the hallway as though our bags weighed nothing.

"That was odd," I told her in a whisper when he was gone.

"It's just Calvin, but be careful," Paige said as she looked around. "Sound carries in this place like you wouldn't believe."

"I whispered, didn't I? What's up with you two, anyway?"

"Nothing," she said, trying to dismiss my question.

I touched her arm lightly. "Paige, that didn't feel like 'nothing' to me."

"The first time we met, he made a clumsy pass at me, and I batted it down a little too harshly for his taste. Since then, we've had a tense relationship, though he never shows it around Aunt Jenny, and I try not to, either." Replacing the frown with a smile, Paige took my hand and pulled me toward a large door to one side. The double doors sported rails and stiles of the same mahogany, but inset within them were nine narrow panels of glass spaced to look like louvers.

"Aunt Jenny. We're here," Paige said as she rushed up to a woman somewhere in her sixties with the loveliest chestnut hair I'd ever seen in my life. It was just beginning to streak with silver, enhancing the richness if it even more, if that were possible. Jenny's hair was definitely her strongest feature, and it captured my attention until I saw her face. She tried to smile for us, but I sensed pain within her, whether physical or mental I couldn't say. *Something* was clearly taking its toll on her, and I started to wonder if that might have been why she'd asked Paige to bring me along.

As Jenny turned to me, I saw the elegance Paige had alluded to. The woman could have been a dancer, the way she moved so gracefully, and I had no doubt that at one point in her life, she had been just that.

There was something almost regal about her, and yet as she neared me, she startled me by embracing me as she had Paige instead of just offering her hand.

I hugged her back, and when she pulled away, I saw a spark in her eyes, if only for a moment. "Forgive me for my familiarity, Suzanne, but Paige has told me so much about you that I feel as though I've known you forever."

"You're forgiven," I said. "I love your home."

"She thinks it should be a museum," Paige told her.

"Paige, did you really have to tell her I said that?" I asked as I turned and lightly scolded my friend.

"Oh, my dear, I agree," Jenny said. "But who would come all the way out here to see it?"

"You'd be surprised," I said. "I don't know how else to ask, so I'll come right out with it. How should I address you? I can't exactly call you Aunt Jenny."

"And why not?" the woman asked with a hint of silver laughter in her voice. "We're kindred spirits, you and I, and Paige has given you her stamp of approval. If you've passed her rigorous examination, then I'm certain you'll pass mine. What do you say?"

"I say I'm honored, Aunt Jenny," I told her.

That bought me another hug.

At least I was ready for it this time.

Paige asked, "Did you want some time alone with Suzanne, Aunt Jenny? I can get us settled in if you do."

"She should stay, Aunt Jenny," I said before she could answer. "You should know that I'm going to bring her up to speed on anything we discuss the second I get the chance. If there's anything you don't want her to know, don't tell me."

"Do you tell *everything* you know to *everyone*?" Jenny asked me, frowning for a moment.

"No, ma'am. Ordinarily, I'm the soul of discretion, but I don't keep things from my husband, and I don't do it from my friends, either. I'm sorry if that doesn't meet with your approval, but it's just the way I am."

Jenny seemed to think about it a moment, and then she nodded once. "Can I trust you, Suzanne?"

"With your life, Aunt Jenny," Paige said.

"I was asking her, dear," Jenny said without taking her gaze off me.

"You can," I told her. "I don't have any way to prove that to you, because anyone can lie, but I give you my word. Anything you tell us, today or in the future, I will not repeat to another soul besides Paige."

"And Jake," she said with a nod.

"How do you know my husband's name?" I asked. "Paige, did you tell her?"

"No, it never came up," Paige answered, looking a bit confused.

"Suzanne, when Paige first mentioned that you were friends, I did some research. You have quite the reputation online."

"You're not talking about as a donutmaker, are you?" I asked her.

"That too," she said, "but now I'm speaking of your amateur sleuthing skills."

"I've had a little luck in the past," I admitted, hedging the truth. "Why? Do you have a problem?"

"Not yet, but after I make my big announcement at dinner tonight, there might be. I thought another set of eyes might be helpful."

"What announcement are you making?" Paige asked her. "Is anything wrong?"

Jenny patted her honorary niece's hand. "All in good time, dear. Now, let's get you two settled before we dine. Things are a bit cramped at the moment despite this house's size, so you two will be sharing the principal suite, if that's all right with you."

"We don't want to dislodge you, Aunt Jenny," I said, stumbling over the new moniker for a moment. That was going to take some getting used to.

"Suzanne, I haven't been able to sleep there since my late husband passed away," she admitted. "I've had two queen beds installed for you and done a bit of redecorating. You should be quite comfortable there."

"That sounds fine with me," I said, glancing at Paige for some kind of clue if it would be fine or not. Her attention was all on her aunt, so I didn't get anything from her.

"Now, if you'll forgive me, I have lots to do before we dine."

"Is there anything we can do to help?" I asked her.

"That's kind of you to offer, but I'll manage fine on my own."

"Just remember, I don't mind earning my keep," I told her.

"Perhaps you could favor us with some of your donuts while you're here. I, for one, am dying to try them after Paige's rave reviews."

"I can do that," I said. "I'm assuming you mean for breakfast tomorrow and not dinner tonight, though I'd be happy either way."

Jenny clasped my hands in hers and laughed. "I knew we'd get along. I just knew it. Tomorrow morning would be just fine."

Paige lingered as I headed for the door, and I saw her whisper something to her aunt, who merely shook her head.

"What was that all about?" I asked my friend once we were back out in the hallway.

"I'm worried about her, Suzanne."

"She's probably just under stress having everyone here," I said, trying my best to reassure her.

"Maybe you're right," she said. "Anyway, if there's something going on, she's clearly not ready to talk about it. Now, let's go check out our room for the next three days."

Chapter 4

The principal suite of the house was bigger than a lot of apartments I'd been in. Not only was there enough room for two queen-sized beds, but there were also huge matching dressers, gorgeous night tables, and even a sitting area, complete with a sofa that was large enough for seven people to lounge around in comfortably. The adjoining bathroom had a large jetted tub as well as a walk-in shower that featured rainwater heads from above and jets coming out of the walls on three sides. Everything was top of the line, even down to the towels and washcloths.

"Wow. I mean, wow," I said as Paige and I finished our tour.

"I know, right?" she asked with a grin. "Aunt Jenny never did anything halfway. This should do, don't you think?"

"You might have trouble getting me to leave," I told her. "What should we do now? Is there time to take a tour of the rest of the house?"

Paige glanced at her watch. "That might have to wait until later. We really should get ready and head downstairs. We should have time for showers if we don't dawdle."

"Okay. Should I wear one of the dresses I brought?"

"I can't imagine Suzanne Hart in a dress," she said with a smile. "I might not recognize you out of your jeans and T-shirt."

"I might not, either," I admitted. "Do you want the bathroom first?"

"No, you go ahead," she said.

I hesitated at the door. "Are you sure I have time for a quick shower?"

"Of course. Just don't take too long. I'd like to grab one too."

"I'll try to restrain myself," I told her as I went in.

It had been harder to pull myself out of that shower than I'd imagined. Not only were there a variety of jets and nozzles, but they came from every direction. The temperature setting was easy to home in to perfection, but I managed to finish with my shower without being urged to vacate by Paige. Wrapping myself up in a luxurious bath-sheet towel made of Egyptian cotton, I used a smaller version for my hair.

"I was just getting ready to evict you," Paige said with a grin. "How was it?"

"Amazing," I told her. "Enjoy."

"I plan to," she replied.

By the time she came out of the bathroom, I was dressed in my second-nicest outfit, a navy-blue midi dress paired with a nice pair of black ankle boots. A bit of jewelry was all I used to accessorize the outfit, a necklace Momma had given me for my twenty-first birthday and some matching earrings she'd provided on my thirtieth. If it weren't for my birthdays, I might not have any jewelry at all, except for the only piece I really cared about, my engagement/wedding ring combo I'd gotten from Jake.

"Wow, you clean up nicely," Paige said as she took in my ensemble.

"Thanks. I like your towel."

"Yeah, I think I'd better up my game for dinner," she answered. "I'm going to have a hard time matching your sense of style."

"I think you'll be just fine. While you're getting dressed, do you mind if I wander around a bit?"

Paige frowned. "It should be fine. Just don't leave this wing."

"Wow, am I under some kind of house arrest or something?" I asked her, half teasing.

"No, I just don't want you running into anyone without having me there by your side," she explained. "You should check out the auxiliary library. It's right next door."

"Do you mean that it's not a part of the main house?" I asked her.

"Oh, there's one there, too, but this was my uncle's private space. It houses the books he loved to read again and again, not the ones that were there mostly for show. I think you'll enjoy it."

"That's an impish little grin you've got there. What do you know that I don't?"

"Suzanne, we don't have time to cover all of *that*," Paige said, and then she broke out into a full-blown grin. We both started laughing, and I left her to get dressed.

I walked out of the room, and after going down the hall a dozen feet, I came to another door.

That had to be it.

When I opened the door, I saw that I had guessed correctly.

There was nothing stuffy about this room. Two comfortable chairs with wonderful direct lights covered the floor space not taken up by bookshelves. A heavy tapestried carpet adorned most of the glistening hardwood floors, and large cherrywood bookcases covered the walls. The only bare spots were for windows and the door I'd come in through. There was nothing as trivial as a painting or a sculpture to detract from the clear and obvious purpose of the room; first and foremost, it was a place to read.

I started browsing the bookshelves at random, and several of my old favorites caught my eye. The first section I found was full of mysteries, sporting cozy authors like MacLeod, Christie, Myers, Hart—a favorite of mine for more reasons than our shared last name—and Cavender, mixed in with the harder Chandler, MacDonald, Leonard, Westlake, and Parker I also adored. Pulling one of my favorite Harts from the shelf, I started leafing through *Death on Demand* and saw that it had been autographed by the author herself. I had a matching one myself, one of my true treasures in life. I'd met Carolyn Hart at a book signing once, and she had been every bit as gracious as I'd hoped she would be. I wished my book club could be there with me now, browsing through this stunning collection of clearly well-read books. These were not the trophies of the well-to-do; they had all clearly been read, loved, and reread again and again.

I was just slipping the novel back onto the shelf when I heard someone behind me.

Thinking it was Paige, I said, "I want to live in this room and read. Bring me something to eat from the party later, would you?"

The laugh I heard wasn't Paige's. It was my hostess's. "My husband used to say the very same thing."

"Oh, forgive me," I told her. "I'm nosy by nature, and I love books almost as much as Paige does."

"That's saying something," Aunt Jenny told me. "This was my husband's favorite room in the entire house."

"I can imagine," I told her. "I'm so sorry for your loss."

"It was years ago, and yet sometimes, it feels as though it all happened yesterday."

She looked more wistful than sad, and I found myself being a bit impertinent, as I could be at times. "How did he pass, if you don't mind my asking?"

"It was his heart. One moment he was fine, sitting in that chair over there, as a matter of fact," she said as she gestured to a seat that had clearly been designed just for reading. "I left to get him some hot chocolate—he hated coffee; cocoa was his passion—and when I came back, he was slumped over in his chair, a Chandler novel in his lap as though he'd been reading and had simply nodded off. I tried to wake him with a kiss, as was my habit, and I knew instantly that something was wrong. He was no longer there, at least the essence of him that mattered to me."

"I didn't mean to bring up a painful memory," I apologized.

"It's not painful at all. I come to this room often. In the entire house, this is where I feel his presence the most. You would have liked him, Suzanne, and I know that he would have gotten along with you."

"I'm sorry we never got the chance to meet, then," I told her earnestly. "How did he feel about donuts?"

She laughed, not a weak chuckle but a full-blown explosion of delight. "He adored them."

"Then I'm *certain* we would have been friends," I answered with a smile.

At that moment, the library door opened. "Did I hear laughter in...oh, hi, Aunt Jenny. I hope it's all right. I told Suzanne she could look around in here. She's almost as big of a mystery nut as I am."

"I'd say we're pretty even," I told her.

"You might just be right," she answered.

"Anyway, I'm sorry if we overstepped our bounds," Paige said.

"Nonsense. Suzanne and I have been having a lovely time. You were right, Paige. She and I are dear and true friends that have simply never met until today."

"I knew you two would hit it off," Paige said.

I was about to reply when there was a single tone that seemed to come out of nowhere.

"That's a reminder from Calvin that dinner will be served in ten minutes. He's a great chef and a decent handyman, but he's got a bit of a temper, so perhaps we'd better go." She glanced at us both, me in my dress and Paige in her dark print skirt and silk top. "You two look like the reason the riot started."

I laughed while Paige nodded. "Uncle Gray used to say the same thing all of the time."

"He was right then, and I'm right now," Aunt Jenny replied.

I commented on her outfit. "You look stunning yourself. I especially like your jewelry. It looks so real." Me and my big mouth. I swear, sometimes I say things without any thought at all.

Jenny laughed. "I should hope so."

"It is? Really?" I asked, taking in the diamonds and emeralds in her necklace, earrings, and the rings adorning her fingers.

"Gray loved to shower me with gifts. I have more modest tastes myself, but it pleased him, so I'm wearing them tonight in his honor and his memory."

I don't know what possessed me, but I took a step forward and hugged her. She seemed a bit surprised at first, but a moment later, she leaned into it. "I'm sure he knows," I said.

"I'm certain as well," Aunt Jenny said. Was that a tear forming in the corner of her eye? It might have been, but she wiped it away so quickly it was hard to say one way or the other. "Let us go into the den of lions and jackals, my dear nieces."

"We're right behind you," my friend said.

As we left the room, Paige lingered a bit and squeezed my hand. "Thank you, Suzanne."

"For what? Coming here with you? I wouldn't have missed it for the world."

"Yes, for that, of course, but mostly for being so kind to Aunt Jenny. She doesn't have enough tenderness in her life."

"She's an amazing woman," I said. "It's not hard being nice to her."

"You'd think so, wouldn't you? Then again, you haven't met the gang we're about to have dinner with. Well, there's no putting it off. It's time."

"I'm ready if you are," I told her, wondering just how bad these people really were.

I had a feeling I was about to find out.

"Ah, Ms. Hart, the famous donutmaking sleuth we've all heard so much about," the bantam Lothario, Frank Palmer, said as he tried to take my hand and kiss it.

I was too quick for him, though. I snatched my fingers away before he got the chance. "Suzanne is fine with me, Mr. Palmer."

"Please. Every time a beautiful woman calls me 'Mister', I die a bit inside."

What a well-oiled and cheesy line, and yet he delivered it with just the right amount of bravado and self-deprecation. It was obvious that I wasn't the first woman he'd ever used it on, nor was I delusional enough to think that it would be the last. "Let me be Frank."

I resisted the urge to comment on his attempt at being clever. "You may," I said as I turned away to the next guest standing nearby, dismissing him as neatly as I could. I saw a cloud of disapproval cross his face, but only for an instant. It seemed that Frank was used to getting a warmer reception than I'd just offered. Well, he was just going to have to live with the disappointment. I had married a real man, at least the second time around, and not some pale imitation foisting himself off as the genuine article.

I offered my hand to the mousy brunette. "You must be Bobbi. It's nice to meet you."

"Hello," she said, taking my hand for a split second before releasing it. "Donuts and detective work. What an exciting life you must lead." There was more than a hint of envy in her voice as she said it.

"Donutmaking is pretty much the same every day," I explained. "Just rinse and repeat with every shift."

"I was referring mainly to the detective work," she explained.

"None of it was by choice," which wasn't completely true. I'd stuck my nose where it didn't belong on more than one occasion, but many of my investigations had been undertaken out of self-preservation. "Besides, that's all behind me," I said, suddenly realizing that I'd finally made up my mind. "I'm retiring from that line of work once and for all."

"But you're at least still going to make donuts, right?" she asked.

"Actually, probably not for long. My assistant and her mother have offered to buy me out, and I'm giving it serious consideration." I hadn't meant to just blurt that out, but evidently, my mouth had other ideas.

"Suzanne. You're not really selling Donut Hearts, are you?" Paige asked me in dismay.

"I just might," I told her. "I can't imagine how many donuts I've made over the years, but it must be in the hundreds of thousands, if not millions."

"Wow, I don't know what I'm going to do if I can't pop across the street and visit you at your shop," she said, clearly upset about the news.

"Donut Hearts will still be there, though I doubt they'll keep the name." That hadn't occurred to me until that moment, but Emma and Sharon would be well within their rights to change it after they bought me out. After all, I was the Hart in the Donut Hearts operation. I was vaguely uneasy about the prospect of it being Blake's Bakery or some variation, but honestly, I couldn't expect them to keep the old name as a legacy for me.

Could I?

"I personally think you should sell it. It sounds like hard, thankless work to me," the voluptuous redhead said.

"You must be Bess," I said as I turned to her.

"I must be, since nobody else here matches my description," she answered, trying to sound coquettish but failing, at least for me. If there was a glimmer of intelligence there, I failed to see it, but then again, if she was smarter than she looked—and honestly, she would just about have to be—then she'd learned to hide it, for whatever reason I couldn't fathom.

"What do you do?" I asked her, genuinely curious.

"You should ask me what I don't do. It's a *much* shorter list," she said, offering that artificial smile again.

I'd had about enough of her, so I turned to the tall, wispy blonde. "That would make you Sandy, then, wouldn't it?"

"It's nice to meet you," Sandy said, taking my hand with a surprisingly strong grip for such a willowy young woman. "I hope we have a chance to chat later."

"Don't you worry. There will be plenty of time for that," Jenny said as a bell from the other room chimed. "Oh dear, Calvin is showing his impatience again. I'm afraid we must go now."

As we filed into the dining room, Paige lingered beside me. "Are you seriously selling Donut Hearts and retiring from detecting too? What are you going to do with your time?"

"Sleep in for a change of pace, maybe?" I asked. "Paige, nothing's been decided for sure about the shop. Can we talk about it later?"

"Sure. I'm sorry. I don't mean to pile on after you went through that gauntlet. You just caught me off guard, that's all."

"The truth is, I kind of surprised myself," I admitted. "Saying it makes it more real somehow."

"Does that mean you might change your mind?" Paige asked me earnestly.

"I might," I admitted.

"But you might not," she added.

I just shrugged as Jenny came back for us.

"Let's go, ladies. There will be time to gossip later. I only have one request: don't start without me. Oh, there's one more thing. If you don't have anything nice to say about somebody, be sure to sit next to me." Our hostess put an arm around each of us and moved us to the dining room. Was she a bit shaky as she walked, or was it because we were all arm in arm? I didn't know, but I meant to find out.

Calvin came in dressed in a chef's outfit, including the tall hat and white jacket, and announced, "Tonight's menu will begin with a crisp autumn medley followed by roast beef tenderloin basted in cognac butter, carrots in crème fraiche, and shredded fire-roasted Brussels sprouts, ending with triple-chocolate cheesecake. I trust you will all enjoy it."

With that, he headed back into what must have been the kitchen, and soon, the last member of the party, Jenny's personal assistant, Roberta, came out with the first course.

It was all magnificent. What Calvin lacked in civility he more than made up for with his offerings. Everything was done to perfection, and I found myself enjoying it all very much, despite the fact that by the time dessert was served, I was fighting off my fatigue. It had been a huge day filled with way too much excitement and change, added to the fact that it was well past my bedtime. That was about to change if I sold Donut Hearts, and I looked forward to the opportunity to stay up past the curfew of a toddler and see what happened after I normally went to sleep every night.

After the last of the dessert dishes had been cleared, Aunt Jenny stood and tapped her water glass for attention, though everyone had been keen on her every word during the entire evening.

She steadied herself for a moment as she stood, tottering a bit until Paige reached out surreptitiously and supported her.

"Thank you, dear," Jenny said softly, and then she turned to her assembled guests. "As you know, I've invited you all here to participate in another Early Inheritance party. For those of you new to the group," she said as she smiled to me, "I take this opportunity every year to award random items from my accumulated wealth to some of you, the group closest to me. This year will be different, though. This is the last time we will be having this party, and the stakes have been raised dramatically because of it."

"Why are you ending it? What's changed?" Frank asked her.

"I don't care to get into that right now," Aunt Jenny said, easily dismissing him. "My reasons are my own. Just know that at the end of these three days, some of my most valuable possessions will be gifted to some of you. As for the grand prize, it will be given at the end of the weekend to the one who will inherit the remainder of my estate upon my passing."

There were some partially hidden smiles, nods, and outright pleasure shown at this announcement, until Bess gestured in my direction. "Surely, Suzanne isn't going to be a part of this," she said. "After all, she's never joined us here before, so it wouldn't be fair. How long have you known her, anyway, Jenny?"

Some of the others nodded in agreement, so before our hostess could say anything, I decided to speak up myself. "Don't worry about it. I have no intention of participating," I said. "After all, we've just met, and I'll happily recuse myself from any and all contests."

"As generous an offer as that is, I'm afraid I can't allow it," Aunt Jenny said strongly and firmly. "The duration of time I've known Suzanne doesn't matter. We are kindred spirits, and she has just as much right to participate in this as any of you. Some might even say more, since her *only* interest seems to be in making me happy."

There were several disclaimers, which she waved away. "In the end, it's my house, my party, and thus, my rules. Anyone unhappy with this arrangement is free to leave right now, before the festivities begin." When no one made a move to go, she nodded. "Just as I thought. Very well. There are six of you, so you know the odds of winning. Oh, there has been another change in the rules. Winning once does not disqualify you from winning again this weekend."

"But that means one person could conceivably get *everything*," Bess said with a pout.

"How perceptive of you," Jenny answered with a slight smile. "Bess, do us all a favor and drop the vapid act, would you, dear? Most of us are well aware that you are quite a bit more intelligent than you admit to."

"She's got you there, Bess," Frank said.

"And Frank," Jenny said, turning her attention to him, "Suzanne has made it painfully clear that she has no interest in anything you are offering, and the other women present have long ago rejected your advances as well. Would it be possible for us to get through this experience *without* having to worry about your wandering eye and hands?"

"I, for one, would appreciate that," Sandy said.

"Really?" Paige asked the quiet woman. "He's tried to corner you too?"

"More times than I can count. I don't consider it an honor, since he doesn't seem to be very discriminating in his choices."

"I can testify to that," Bobbi added. "Yes, he's even hit on me a time or two, if you can believe that."

"All right, if we're finished bashing the lone male present that is a guest and not staff, could we please move on to another topic?" Frank asked as he looked around the room. He then said, "Jenny, you've taken shots at Bess and me. You really should play fair and go after the others as well."

"There's nothing she can say about me," Sandy said meekly.

"Really? Are you absolutely certain that you want to stick with that line of defense?" Aunt Jenny asked, her gaze piercing in nature as if she knew something the rest of us didn't.

Sandy merely shook her head and put her chin down, letting her hair mostly hide her face. "No. I'm sorry. I was wrong."

Jenny nodded and then turned to Bobbi, who put her hands up in the air in surrender before our hostess could speak. "Trust me, you can't say anything I haven't been thinking about myself for years. I'm nobody who means nothing."

"You haven't always felt that way, though, have you?" Jenny asked, not relenting with that gaze.

"No," she stammered. "Not always."

"What about Paige and Suzanne?" Bess asked. "They can't be the *only* good folks here."

"I'm the first to admit that I have more than my share of flaws," Paige answered quickly, "but then again, I never pretended otherwise. As for Suzanne, she isn't perfect either, but she's the best friend I could ask for, and when the chips are down, she's someone I know that I can count on."

"Thanks," I said as I reached across the table and squeezed her hand.

"I meant every word of it," she said.

"Even the part where you said I wasn't perfect?" I asked, pretending to be distressed by the question.

Paige grinned at me, I smiled back, and then we started laughing.

Only Jenny chimed in and joined us.

"Fine. We're all human," Frank said. "Now that we've all taken off our masks, when does this new party start?"

Jenny looked at him oddly. "I'm sorry. I thought you realized it.

"It already has."

Chapter 5

"The first test will examine how observant you all are. In the drawing room, Roberta has been setting up a scene for all of you while we've been dining. You will be allowed one minute in the room, entering through the hallway and exiting out onto the back patio. There will be no sharing, no consulting, no conversation at all between any of you until a winner has been declared. Once you've exited the room, you will find six pads of paper and a list of ten identical questions. Whoever answers the most questions correctly will win. Once you've finished, deposit your answers in the locked box on the table and go to the ballroom. Under no circumstances are any of you allowed to come back here. Do you all understand and agree to these terms and conditions?"

Quizzes and tests must have been part of the regular routine of the Early Inheritance parties, because no one had any questions or concerns. I didn't have any, either, but mostly because I had no idea what was going on. I'd do my best, not just because I wanted to win but because I wanted to please Aunt Jenny. I had only known her for a few hours, but I'd already found her to be a dear friend. It was like that sometimes. It could take me months, if not years, to warm up to some folks, while others, I took to immediately. Our hostess was definitely in the latter group.

Aunt Jenny motioned to Calvin, who brought out a large crystal bowl and placed it on a quarter-sawn oak table. "Your names are in here, so they will be drawn at random. Good luck, everyone."

I found myself hoping that my name would be drawn last to give me some time to prepare myself, but just my luck, I was chosen first.

"Good luck," Jenny said as she squeezed my hand. "Knock 'em dead, Suzanne."

"Thanks," I said as I headed down the hallway to the drawing room, whatever that was.

Roberta was waiting for me there. I smiled at her, but she didn't return it. "You have one minute. You can't touch anything, move anything, or adjust anything. You are to stay on the red carpet and move through the room without straying. I will be watching you the entire time from this monitor," she said as she tapped a screen I hadn't noticed, "so don't even think about disobeying the rules. Your minute starts right now."

I nodded and walked through the door, wondering what I was about to see.

It was certainly nothing I'd been expecting.

The room had been set up like one of those old I Spy games I'd played in books as a kid. There were compasses hidden in the woodwork, a wind-rose woven into the draperies, a ladybug sitting on a red-and-black couch, a knife sticking out of a pillow cushion and a thousand other things either hidden, partially hidden, or disguised altogether. A large digital clock stood over the exit, counting the seconds down to my exit. I took everything in that I could, but my brain was on overload by the time the clock neared ten seconds. I'd wondered how I'd know when my time was up when an automated voice began a countdown, too, just in case I'd somehow failed to notice the clock. As I walked to the exit, I glanced up at the clock and saw that it had been made by Timothy's Time and Temperature, a brand I'd never heard of before. The nameplate had been so ornately crafted with scrolling script that I nearly overstayed my welcome puzzling out the letters.

I got out just in time, though, and I heard the door automatically lock behind me.

That had been close!

Grabbing a pen and a pad, I started working immediately.

"Where was the yellow grasshopper?"

What? I hadn't seen a grasshopper in the entire room, let alone a yellow one. Could it have been in the yellow sunburst painting over the mantel? That was the only yellow spot in the room. I thought about putting it down as a guess, but then I decided that if I wasn't certain, I wouldn't guess, at least not at this point.

I wrote, "There was no yellow grasshopper."

I was probably wrong, but at least I put something down.

"Where was the wind-rose located?"

I knew that one, at least.

I kept going through the questions until I got to the last one.

"What was the brand name of the digital clock above the door?"

Hah. I knew that too! I wrote the name down, studied my sheet again, then folded it and started to put it into the box. It was almost completely gone when I realized that I hadn't put my name on my entry!

Snatching it back, I quickly wrote, "Suzanne Hart Bishop" and then deposited it again.

That had been fun, but I didn't have a prayer of winning. Two answers had given me fits, the yellow grasshopper and the number of teacups on the back table. There had been either ten or eleven, but I hadn't been sure. Breaking my rule of not guessing, I put down eleven, but after I deposited my answer sheet, I was certain that I had been wrong. After all, who would have a tea set with eleven cups? Twelve maybe, even ten, but eleven? Oh, well, I'd done my best. I made my way to the ballroom, following the signs, and I found a nice room that wasn't really big enough for a ball, but it could have held a small dance, at any rate. I looked around at the artwork until I heard someone enter the room behind me.

It was Paige!

"You were second in line?" I asked. "Oh, are we allowed to talk now, or is the rule of silence still in effect?"

Paige put a finger to her lips, and I shut up instantly. Honestly, these games should have come with a booklet of instructions, though everyone else probably already knew them by heart.

One by one, spaced a minute between their appearances, everyone else joined us in our silent vigil. Ten more minutes passed until Jenny came in, holding a jewelry box the size of a large book in her hands.

"After scoring the results, I'm pleased to announce that we have a clear winner in the weekend's first contest," Jenny said. "With a perfect score of ten out of ten, the winner is Suzanne."

"What?" I asked loudly. There were immediate grumbles from some of the others, but I chose to ignore them. Paige was the only one who looked remotely happy that I'd won. "But I didn't find the yellow grasshopper, and I put eleven teacups down when I'm pretty sure there were more or less than that."

Jenny laughed. "As it turns out, both answers were correct. There were two sheets with scores of eight, but you were the only one to identify the clock manufacturer correctly *and* the number of teacups. Congratulations, Suzanne," she said as she stepped toward me and opened the substantial box.

It was a magnificent necklace with a lovely diamond in the center surrounded by a starburst of emeralds. I couldn't believe it was real.

"Seriously? She gets the Mattingly piece?"

"I'm sorry. It has a *name*?" I asked as I tried to take it in.

"That necklace was commissioned for Sarah Ann Mattingly by one of the Fremont brothers, who was trying to woo her in the early 1900s,"

Bess explained. "She doesn't even know what it's worth," she complained to Jenny.

"I know. Isn't it refreshing? Suzanne, step forward, please."

I did as she asked, and my honorary Aunt Jenny placed the jewelry around my neck. Though it was fairly streamlined and it lay flat against my chest, I could feel the weight of it instantly, and as I looked down at it, the center diamond seemed to be lit with an internal fire.

"It looks lovely on you, my dear," Aunt Jenny said. "I hope you enjoy it."

"I don't know what to say," I told her, almost as speechless as I ever got.

"I require nothing more than a simple word of thanks," she said with a wry smile.

"Thank you," I said as I pivoted and hugged her again.

"You are most welcome. Wear it in good health," Jenny answered. As she handed me the box the piece had come in, she spoke to the rest of the group gathered together. "Why the long faces?" she asked. "This is the first of several prizes to be given before the grand finale. There's plenty of opportunity for all of you to win if you're clever enough."

"Or lucky enough," Frank murmured under his breath.

Jenny might not have been feeling all that well, but there was nothing wrong with her hearing. "Luck had nothing to do with it," she answered with a false sweetness.

"Of course not," Frank answered, putting on a brave face. "Well done, Suzanne. I must say, it looks amazing on you."

"Thanks," I answered. I turned to Jenny. "It's a bit heavy even though it's not bulky, isn't it?"

She laughed, and not a polite little chuckle, either, but one with true feeling. "I found it so myself. That's one reason I've rarely worn it over the years. If you like, I can put you in contact with one of my jewelers in New York, who will make sure you get a fair price for it."

"It's a gift," I said, putting my hands on my prize. "I wouldn't show you disrespect like that."

"I appreciate the sentiment. Tell you what. Keep it this weekend, and then we'll talk on Sunday evening before you leave. If you enjoy it for the next few days, I'll be more than satisfied. How does that sound?"

"Do I need to wear it the entire time?" I asked her, realizing what a burden it could be and instantly feeling bad about my reaction. Here she'd given me something probably worth more than my donut shop, and I was already considering it an inconvenience.

"Goodness, no. Let me take it off for you." After she undid the clasp, she placed it back in its case. "Keep it on your dresser and admire it from time to time. That's all I ask."

"I can do that," I said. "Are you sure you want to let it go?" It was truly lovely, but I felt bad taking it, especially after knowing Jenny only hours instead of the months and years the rest of the gathering had known her.

"I'm positive. The look of surprise on your face is more than I hoped for, and I couldn't be happier that you won."

"Thanks again."

"Suzanne, enough thanks. There will be plenty of other opportunities for you to win again, and I don't want you to use up all of your gratitude when we've barely gotten started."

"Okay," I said sheepishly. I tried not to look at the other folks in the room, but it was hard not to feel the sheer amount of hatred and animosity being directed toward me.

I tucked the jewelry box under one arm as Paige and I got some of the champagne Roberta served.

"This is crazy," I told Paige softly once we'd moved to the side, out of earshot of the others. "I can't accept this." After a moment's pause, I added, "Can I?"

"You heard Aunt Jenny. She wants you to have it. Suzanne, you protested, she overruled you, and that's the last she wants to discuss it.

When Aunt Jenny makes up her mind about something, she doesn't go back. Ever."

"It's got to be expensive, though. I'm not even sure I can afford the insurance on it," I said.

"If I were you, I'd do as she suggested. Enjoy it this weekend, and come Sunday, let the jeweler sell it for you. It should make your decision about selling Donut Hearts easier."

"How's that?" I asked, unsure of what she meant.

"Well, with the proceeds from the sale, you won't have to sell the business at all."

"I'm not doing it for the money," I answered. "I believe I can see the end of my donutmaking career, whether I have money or not."

"Wow, you really are considering selling it, aren't you?"

"I am," I told her. "But I'm not like Aunt Jenny. I reserve the right to change my mind at any time."

Paige was about to answer when Aunt Jenny said, "If you'll all excuse me, I'm going to wish you a good night. Suzanne, would you mind walking me to my room?"

"Of course not," I said as I glanced at Paige. She nodded her approval, though I felt bad about cutting her out of her aunt's affections, even if it was only for a moment.

"I'll be in our room," Paige said as she touched my shoulder lightly and smiled.

"Thanks," I said.

Aunt Jenny put a hand on my shoulder as we walked out of the room, and I could feel her weight on me. "Take my arm," I said.

She did as I suggested, and I walked her down the hallway to a modest room tucked away from the other bedrooms of the house. "Do you stay here all of the time?" I asked her.

"As a matter of fact, it's the maid's quarters, but it suits me," Aunt Jenny said with a grin.

"I know you said you couldn't stay in the master suite anymore, and I completely understand that, but surely, any of the other bedrooms has to be nicer than this." The room was modest by any stretch of the definition, with simple pine Shaker-style furniture, though not much of it. There was a simple bedframe, a plain dresser, a nightstand, and a chair, and that was about it. The space was small, but it did look homey. "It kind of reminds me of the servants' quarters at the Biltmore house in Asheville," I told her without thinking. "I'm sorry. That's probably not the right thing to say." The Biltmore house was the largest private residence in the United States, built by the Vanderbilt family in the late 1800s.

"That's exactly what I was going for," she said, pleased with the comparison. "I always preferred the servants' quarters over the main bedrooms."

"Me too," I said.

"I have no trouble believing that," she said.

As I helped her settle onto the edge of the bed, I asked, "Aunt Jenny, may I ask you something?"

"It appraised at seventy-five thousand dollars, but that was a few years ago. I have no doubt you'll get over a hundred thousand for it in today's market."

"No, that's not what I wanted to know, but wow. That's just crazy."

"It is, isn't it? What's your question, my dear? I'm weary from all of the excitement, and I need to rest."

"Are you feeling okay?" I asked. "I'm worried about you."

She reached out and took my hand in hers. "I'm fine."

"We haven't been friends long, but there's something you should know about me," I told her sternly. "I hate being lied to, especially by people I care about. What's really going on?"

"It's simple enough," she said after giving it a moment's consideration. "I'm dying, Suzanne, and there's nothing anyone can do about it."

Chapter 6

"What do you mean, you're dying?" I asked her as I slumped down on the bed beside her. "Are you sure?"

Aunt Jenny patted my hand. "I am, as well as the seven doctors I've consulted with over the past year. I'm afraid there's no mistaking the diagnosis. I won't make you ask. I've got cancer, one I'd never heard of before it struck me. Evidently, it's a rare one, so woohoo, lucky me."

"I'm so sorry," I said. "Are you in much pain?"

"It's sweet of you to ask. No, it's nothing I can't manage without more than some mild over-the-counter medication. It's mostly robbed me of my energy, and I'm told it will just get worse and worse before the end."

"So should you really be having this party? Why don't you send everyone home? Paige and I can stay if you'd like some company, but if that's too taxing, we can leave as well."

"No. Absolutely not," she said firmly, showing some of that backbone and stubbornness Paige had told me about. "This weekend has given me something to look forward to when I desperately needed it, and I won't have it ruined for anything. Do we understand each other?"

I felt like a schoolgirl being reprimanded for being tardy. "Yes, ma'am. I'm sorry. I didn't mean to overstep my boundaries."

"Don't apologize," she said, brightening up again instantly. "It's going to be such fun."

"For you, maybe, but your guests seemed pretty miserable, especially after I won the contest tonight."

"It was my fondest hope when I suggested to Paige that she bring you," Aunt Jenny said.

"I really won, though, right?" I asked, having a suspicion that the game might have been rigged in my favor. "It was fair and square." I wouldn't be able to accept the prize if I believed for an instant that it wasn't.

"The integrity of my contests is sacrosanct," Aunt Jenny told me firmly, and I believed her.

"So, there really *wasn't* a yellow grasshopper?" I asked her with a giggle.

"No, but you should have read some of the creative answers I got to a question that had no answer," she answered.

"That was a bit cruel. Funny, but cruel," I told her.

"That's exactly what I meant it to be. I'm sure you've been wondering why I've gathered this particular group of people together, when none of them, with the exceptions of you and Paige, seem to like me even just a little."

"I'd be lying if I told you that the thought hadn't crossed my mind," I admitted.

"You'll just have to trust me that there's a reason each of my guests garnered an invitation this weekend," she said.

"Care to give me any specifics?" I asked her.

She sighed a bit and then shook her head. "We'll save that conversation for another time. If I'm going to be ready for tomorrow's events, I need to get my rest."

"Of course," I said. "Is there anything I can do for you?"

"As a matter of fact, there is. Don't treat me like an invalid or even someone who is dying. After all, we all are going to suffer the same end. Some sooner than others, but no one gets out of this thing we call life alive."

"I can't argue with that," I said, forcing a smile when I didn't feel one. "I'll do my best to respect your wishes. All of them."

"That's my girl," Aunt Jenny said.

"You know I'm going to tell Paige the second I get back to our room, right?"

"I really wish you wouldn't," she said with a frown.

"I told you from the start. No secrets." Clearly, Aunt Jenny could be stubborn, but there was something she needed to know about me. In a contest of sheer mulishness, I was, at the very least, her match.

"Do me a favor. You may tell her, but wait until Sunday. Please? It's important she not know this weekend."

"I'm sure she already suspects you aren't well," I told her.

"Give me this at least. It's the request of a dying woman, Suzanne. How can you refuse me that?"

I wanted to tell her that my code of ethics couldn't be bent, let alone broken, but I just couldn't do it. "Wow. Well played. Fine. But if you don't tell her Sunday, I'm going to, necklace or no necklace."

"I respect that," she said. "Thank you."

"That's enough thank-yous for one night between us, don't you think?" I asked her with a grin.

"More than enough," she said. "May I make one more request?"

"Wow, give a girl a diamond-and-emerald necklace, and the requests never stop," I said with a grin.

"I didn't mean to impose."

"Aunt Jenny, I'm kidding. I've got a sense of humor not many people get, but I've learned to live with it. I'll do anything for you within my power, and not because of your generous gift. Once you are a friend of mine, it's nearly impossible to shake me off."

"I'm the exact same way myself," she answered. "I know I asked you before, but I'm afraid you didn't think I really meant it. Would it be too much trouble to make donuts for us in the morning?"

"No trouble at all. I have a difficult time sleeping in even on my days off," I admitted. "Yeast or cake donuts?"

"Is yes a possible answer to that question?" she asked, and for a moment, I could see how she must have been as a small child.

I had to laugh. "Of course it is."

"Oh, and Calvin will be assisting you in the kitchen."

"Thanks, but I don't need any help," I told her. Having him in the kitchen was not my idea of a good time, especially if he was watching me like a hawk.

"He's heard about your donuts, and he'd love to learn from you," she said. "Please? As a favor to me?"

"Why not?" I asked, feeling it impossible to say no to this woman.

"Excellent. Good night, then."

"Good night."

I almost asked her how long she had left, but I couldn't bring myself to do it. We'd found a way to get through it, and I didn't want to tire her any more. I felt bad about keeping anything from Paige, but I couldn't find it in my heart to refuse Aunt Jenny's request.

We were going to share one secret between us, at least for a bit, and I was going to have to find a way to be okay with that.

"I've been dying to ask you something. May I try it on?" Paige asked as I walked into our room.

"Of course," I said, "but I'm not sure how it's going to look with your pajamas."

She'd changed into the cutest pair of white-and-black Holstein cow pajamas while I'd been gone, something that I was envious of, since wearing a dress was by no means my usual attire. As I handed her the box and grabbed my own jammies, she said, "I think this would look good on me if it was *all* I was wearing."

"Can you at least wait till I'm in the bathroom changing before you strip down and parade around the room with only that on?" I asked her with a grin.

"I'll try to restrain myself," Paige said with an answering smile as she put it on over her cow pajamas. "See? It looks good even in these."

"It's pretty crazy," I said. "Enjoy it."

When I came back out, changed and ready for bed, I saw that she'd taken the necklace off and restored it to its box. "That thing will break your back, won't it? How can it be so flat and still so heavy?"

"I have no idea. You could wear it under your shirt, and no one would even know you had it on. It's a workout, though, there's no doubt about it," I said.

"So, what did you and Aunt Jenny talk about? You were gone forever," Paige asked me.

"Sorry about that. I felt bad you weren't included."

"Don't. The two of us have lots of time to spend together this weekend, even with the jackals in residence," Paige answered.

"Well, I'd love to stay up and chat the night away, but I'm getting up early and making donuts in the morning."

"But it's your weekend off," Paige protested. "You should get to sleep in at least until six or seven."

"Aunt Jenny asked, and I really don't mind, but if it's all the same to you, I'm going to crash."

"It's fine. I brought my e-reader, so I'm all set," she said. "You never answered my question."

"How about that?" I asked.

When she saw that I wasn't going to give her a straight answer, Paige said, "Don't worry about waking me when you get up tomorrow. I sleep like the dead up here in the mountains."

"That's good to know," I answered. I debated slipping into the bathroom and calling Jake to tell him about my windfall, but I decided it could wait. I was tired, and it was going to be time to get up before I knew it. Besides, going to sleep early meant that I didn't have to lie to Paige about her aunt's condition any more that night. I'd have trouble fulfilling that promise, but I was determined to keep Aunt Jenny's secret safe.

After all, let Paige have these next three days in blissful ignorance. Sunday would be here soon enough.

Chapter 7

I didn't sleep well, which wasn't all that unusual on my first night away from home, but this had nothing to do with the unfamiliar setting. A massive storm full of thunder and lightning kept pounding away at the night with its artillery fire, and it would have been a wonder if any of us had gotten any rest.

As I left the room a little after two a.m., stumbling around in the darkness, my hand touched the jewelry box Aunt Jenny had given me the night before. For a moment, I thought it had been just a dream, but that box made it real. I wanted to look at the bauble again just to be sure, but I didn't want to wake Paige. She was breathing heavily, sound asleep, but I hadn't even needed the alarm on my phone to wake me. Old habits died hard. If I sold the shop to Emma and Sharon, would I ever get used to sleeping in like other folks did? I wasn't sure, but I was certainly willing to give it a shot. I was still feeling the remnants of the burrito food poisoning I'd gotten with Grace, and somehow, it just made me miss her even more. How was I ever going to get by without her? Pushing down the feelings, I left the suite and headed for the kitchen, hoping that Calvin had decided to sleep in after all.

"You're up," I told Calvin when I walked into the lit kitchen.

"I'm sorry. Didn't Jen tell you I would be?" he asked, clearly confused by my statement.

"She told me. I just didn't think she was serious. Calvin, I've tasted your food, remember? Based on what I sampled last night, I know you can outcook me any day of the week and twice on Sundays."

"Maybe in dinner fare, but I've never been able to make a decent donut, cake or yeast, and I've tried. Listen, I know how I come off most of the time, but I really would love to learn from you. I promise not to get in your way, and I'll try to keep my questions to a minimum."

"Sorry, but that's not going to work for me," I told him. His look of disappointment was too much to take, so I quickly added, "You need to ask me any question that comes to mind, no matter how basic or silly it might feel asking it, and if you're going to learn, the only way to do it is to get your hands dirty. Well, floury anyway. What do you say? Can you live with my demands?"

His grin was open, honest, and, I had to believe, sincere. "Yes, ma'am. I'm going to take notes, if you don't mind."

"I do it all of the time. In fact, I've got a book full of recipes, both successes and failures, that I've been updating since I started making donuts years ago."

"Any chance I could take a look at it?" he asked, clearly coveting it the moment he heard me describe it.

"I wish I could, but I left it back in April Springs. Don't worry, though, what we're going to be doing today I could do in my sleep. Let's start with the yeast donuts. I assume you're well provisioned here."

"You're going to love this," he said with a grin as he led me back into what turned out to be a pantry.

Calvin must have been a morning person, because the change in him from what I'd seen the night before was startling. Before we got to the pantry, I said, "You seem different today."

"You mean I'm not a total jerk?" he asked me with a smile.

"Exactly," I said. "Okay, I would have put it a little more delicately, but it's true. What was up with you last night?"

"I get overprotective when it comes to Jen," he explained. "I tried to talk her out of this weekend, but she wouldn't listen to me. I knew it would be a strain on her, and we had just had a tiff about it before you and Paige arrived."

"Are you in love with her?" I asked, taking a stab in the dark.

His reaction surprised me. The laughter was too strong, too involved, to be anything but true amusement at my question. "She's like the mother I never had," he told me. "Not that I didn't have a mother, but she wasn't cut out for the job, you know? Jen saw through my rough façade and gave me a job and a reason to be. I owe her everything. But romance? Nope. Not a chance."

"Hey, I'm sorry. It was a fair question."

"I suppose so," he replied.

"How about you and Paige?" I wanted to hear his side of the story.

"That's a little more complicated," he said, neatly ducking the question. "Check this out. Do we have what you need?" Calvin opened a door, and I saw what paradise looked like to a chef, a cook, a baker, or just about anybody who liked to create food. Neatly organized, there were foodstuffs from across the world, some of which I'd only read about in my fanciest cookbooks.

"It's a bit overwhelming, isn't it?"

"It still has that effect on me," Calvin admitted as he handed me a basket. "If you need anything and don't see it, just ask. As a matter of fact, tell me what you need, and I'll pull it from the shelves for you," he added as he took the basket back.

I told him what I needed as I checked things off my mental list, and Calvin gathered them, from three kinds of flour to yeast to sugar to salt to a dozen other items. Each was the best that money could buy. This was going to be fun.

After we set things up on the counter, Calvin asked, "Do you ever make small batches, or are we going to do a full run?"

It was my turn to laugh. "We'd fill up the dining room with donuts, and Aunt Jenny would think I'd lost my mind."

"Don't kid yourself. She'd love it," he said with a slight smile. "I noticed that you called her Aunt Jenny last night. Was that her idea or yours?"

"Strictly hers," I said quickly. "I don't know, there are some people, when you meet them, it feels as though they're longtime friends you've just never seen before. That's the way we clicked."

"I know. I could see it in the way she looked at you. She's a fan, Suzanne."

"No more than I am of hers," I countered. "Let's scale my recipes back some. What kind of oil do you have for frying?"

"Peanut, canola, vegetable, olive, and coconut."

"Excellent. I've recently switched to peanut oil, and I love it. Let's get started on the yeast donuts first. While they're rising, we can do the cake donuts. Do you mind grabbing the peanut oil and putting six inches of it into a large pot? We need it at 365 degrees F."

Calvin grinned at me, and then it suddenly hit me. "I'm sorry. It's an old habit. I'm treating you like an assistant, not a chef in your own right."

"I thought it was cute. As a matter of fact, I'd be happy to be your assistant for today."

"We can at least call you my sous chef," I said with a grin.

"I'll take it," Calvin replied as he did as I asked. "Don't do anything until I've finished putting the oil on."

"I won't," I told him.

Once he was ready, I made the batter up for my general cake donut mix in a substantial stand mixer that sat on the counter. Calvin took it all in, writing everything down as I went but still managing to watch my every move. Once the generic batter was finished mixing, I asked for and received four smaller bowls. Dividing up the batter, I explained, "We're making four kinds of cake donuts with the same basic recipe.

One will be plain cake, one chocolate, one cherry, and the last one, I'll let you pick. Does Aunt Jenny have a favorite flavor?"

"She loves apple cider," he said.

"I'm guessing you have cider on hand," I told him.

"Always," he admitted.

"Then that's our last donut flavor." I showed him how to mix the appropriate amounts of cocoa powder, dried cherries, and apple cider into each of the respective batches. Only the first bowl remained pristine.

"I don't suppose you have a donut ring dropper, do you?" I asked, betting that he didn't. "It's okay. I can use two spoons to scoop them out. They just won't be as pretty."

"How about this?" he asked as he pulled out a donut dropper nicer than any I'd ever seen before. "Will this do?"

"It's perfect," I said as I took it. "This place has everything."

"Don't be too impressed. Jen had one express shipped here yesterday when she asked Paige to invite you."

"Still, it was pretty thoughtful," I said as I loaded the dropper up with the plain batter first. After double-checking the oil temperature, I dropped the first three rings into the pot and watched the donuts sizzle beautifully. When it was time to flip them, Calvin offered me a wire mesh spider, but I preferred bamboo skewers, which I'd nabbed earlier from one of the kitchen tool drawers.

He had the cooling rack ready for me, and as the donuts came out, I laid them on it to drain the last bits of oil. Whipping up a plain glaze, I hit half of them while they were still warm and then repeated the process for each of the other flavors of donuts we made. Calvin took it all in, and once everything was glazed and starting to cool, he asked, "Did you make enough for us to sample them?"

"Nobody out there is going to know how many we made," I said, emphasizing the "we." "Help yourself."

He grinned like a schoolboy and broke an apple cider donut in half, giving me part of it. After a bite, he turned to me and shook his head. "You make it look so easy. How do you do it?"

"You can make these every bit as well as I can," I told him.

"I doubt that," he replied.

"Try making a few hundred thousand. You'll get the hang of it eventually," I said as I laughed. I'd been dreading having him in the kitchen with me, but it was turning out to be a nice morning, nicer because of his presence, not in spite of it. After we sampled the others, I pronounced them good enough to serve, and he concurred.

Before we got started on the next phase of the yeast donuts, I asked, "Do you and Roberta resent not being included in these treasure hunts Aunt Jenny is hosting?"

"No way," he said without hesitation. "She's provided for us already, both now and after she's gone."

"Good. I'm sorry if I'm nosy, but it's kind of who I am."

"I don't mind," he said. "Though don't tell the others what I'm really like. I kind of enjoy making them squirm."

"Your secret is safe with me," I said, realizing that I shouldn't say anything to Paige, either. Wow, the secrets were really piling up between us, and when she found out what I'd kept from her, I hoped she'd be able to forgive me.

"Thanks. Now, what's next?" he asked eagerly.

I showed him how to finish the yeast donuts and even let him cut a few himself and drop them into the oil. He did it expertly, which didn't surprise me at that point. The man really did know his way around a kitchen.

The yeast donuts turned out great as well, and after learning that Aunt Jenny loved chocolate-glazed peanut donuts, I made a batch just for her after I made my other glazes and icing toppings. "I hope nobody has peanut allergies out there," I said.

"Frank is allergic to seafood, and Bess can't have soy milk."

"And you'd know that because you're cooking for the group," I said as I nodded. "I probably should have asked you before I started topping these."

"I would have stopped you, or at least let you know," he said.

Once we were finished with everything, I started to clean up.

"No, ma'am," Calvin said. "As your sous chef, that's my responsibility. Remember, you're still a guest here, after all."

"I don't mind," I told him, ignoring his command.

"Jen would be upset, though. Do you really want to be responsible for that?"

"Wow, you fight dirty," I said as I tossed the dishcloth in my hand at him.

He caught it deftly and smiled. "You don't know the half of it. Now, would you like to wheel out the cart that's filled with some of your creations?"

"It was a team effort," I told him. "You can do it for us."

"I'm not sure that's such a great idea, but if I do, they're going to know the truth. I got in your way more than anything."

"I don't agree with that. I've got to say, this was fun."

"It was," he answered, "but don't forget, I'm an aloof jerk as far as everyone but you and Jen are concerned. Agreed?"

"Agreed," I replied. "Maybe you'd better let me push that cart in after all. I wouldn't want anyone to think you were doing me any favors."

"That's the spirit," Calvin said with a grin. "Thanks. I really appreciate the donutmaking lessons. I learned a ton of new techniques."

"It was nothing," I answered.

"No, ma'am. It was the opposite of nothing."

"It was *everything*?" I asked him innocently. "I don't see how that could be."

"You've got a bite yourself, don't you?" he asked me as he smiled.

"*You* are the one who has no idea," I told him as I bid him farewell and wheeled the laden cart out into the dining room to serve my fellow guests.

Chapter 8

I'd been expecting an empty dining room. After all, it was still early. But to my surprise, everyone was there, including Aunt Jenny. "Wow, this is quite the reception," I said.

"Aunt Jenny made it a point that everyone needed to be up and ready to eat by the time you finished the donuts," Paige said.

"It's only fair, dear," Aunt Jenny said, looking a bit better than she had the night before. She really had needed the rest. Maybe it wasn't as bad as she thought. Okay, that was pure wishful thinking on my part, but hey, I'd grown really fond of the lady in a very short time. "You've been up all night making donuts for us. It's the least we can do."

"Actually, I slept in until two a.m.," I replied.

"And you do that *every* morning?" Sandy asked me incredulously.

"I did it seven days a week when I opened my shop. Over the years, I've been having my assistant and her mother take over more and more. I'm down to four or five days a week now."

"Still, it's more than I would be willing to do," Bobbi answered.

"Yes, let's all agree that Suzanne is amazing. I'm starving. May we eat now?" Frank asked.

I laughed, more at his hurt tone of voice than anything else. "By all means. I've already sampled the offerings today, along with Calvin."

"How did that go?" Aunt Jenny asked me softly.

I nearly told the truth until I caught myself. "You know Calvin," I said, winking at her when no one else was watching.

She got it, but no one else did. "That deserves combat pay, working alongside that insufferable man," Bess said.

"What's wrong, Bess, didn't *he* succumb to your charms?" Frank asked with a nasty little laugh.

"Please, it's too early to start sniping at each other," Sandy said.

"Is it *ever* too early for that?" Frank asked.

"What have we here?" Aunt Jenny asked as she looked at the offerings on the cart.

"I've brought out a sampling, so there's some of everything, but there are more in the kitchen if we run low. Aunt Jenny, I made you apple cider cake donuts and chocolate-covered peanut yeast donuts. I understand those are your favorites."

"You shouldn't have," our hostess said with a broad grin that was more suited for a kid than a dying woman, something that gave me great pleasure. "But I'm glad you did." She took a bite of the cider donut first. "This is incredible. I hope you taught Calvin how to make these."

"He's a quick study," I told her. "Any time you want them, all you have to do is ask. He wrote down the recipes."

"I'm going to weigh three hundred pounds," Aunt Jenny said with a grin as she dug into a chocolate peanut donut. I'd applied the chocolate especially thick, and there were so many peanuts encrusted in the topping it was tough to see the rich darkness underneath. "These are amazing. You've outdone yourself, Suzanne."

"Well, since you've never had my donuts before, that wouldn't be tough to do," I said. "Come on, everybody, dig in. There should be something here for everybody."

They each took a single donut, with the exception of Paige. "I've had her treats before. I'm not going to bother coming back later." She grabbed a plain cake, a cherry cake, and an apple cider donut for herself.

"Wow, it must be so freeing not to have to worry about how much you eat," Bess said to her, clearly taking a shot at Paige, though my friend sported a petite figure that never seemed to vary much from year to year.

"It is," she said with a grin as she took a huge bite from the cider donut. "Man, I've missed these."

"Don't you usually eat donuts at Suzanne's shop?" Aunt Jenny asked her.

"Oh, yes, but the apple cider ones are rare treats. She holds back pumpkin donuts, apple cider ones, and red velvet for special occasions."

"I find it creates a sense of scarcity if I offer some flavors intermittently. Besides, if I tried to make every donut I've ever made every single day, I wouldn't be able to start serving until noon."

"That makes perfect sense," Aunt Jenny approved.

As folks started in on their donuts, they added beverages from the bar Roberta had set up that offered a range from coffee and hot tea to three kinds of milk—plain, chocolate, and, to my delight, strawberry. There were also choices of apple, orange, and cranberry juice as well, but there were no other main courses besides my donuts. I was afraid the entire group was going to have a sugar rush from all the sweets. I *never* recommended a steady diet of my donuts. They were a great treat, but you couldn't, or at least shouldn't, live off them.

Calvin came out to restock the trays with more donuts, and he nodded to me as he did so. "I understand you did a nice job helping with the donuts," Aunt Jenny told him.

"She made everything. I just watched and took notes. If they're not very good, it's all her fault." He turned and winked at me so no one else could see him. I could swear I caught Aunt Jenny smiling, but it was gone as quickly as it had appeared.

Paige wasn't in on the joke. "I'll have you know Suzanne has won awards for her donuts, Calvin."

"Come on, I placed second in the county fair with my pumpkin iced crullers one year," I told her. "That hardly counts as being award winning."

"You got a ribbon, didn't you?"

"Sure, but it was red, not blue," I told her.

"Well, I think they're delightful," Aunt Jenny said, though I noticed that she'd only taken small bites of each of her two favorite donuts, and then she'd broken them up and pushed them around on her plate to make it appear that she'd eaten more than she really had. Apparently, our hostess was sicker than she looked. I wasn't feeling that great myself from my bout of food poisoning, but at least I'd gotten some of my appetite back. Maybe I was finally getting over whatever had ailed me before.

After we were finished eating, Aunt Jenny said, "Suzanne, thank you again for providing us with our morning meal. They were truly excellent."

"Thank you. It was my pleasure."

"I don't mean to complain, but aren't we getting anything else to eat, something more substantial?" Frank asked. "Don't get me wrong, the donuts were good, but I was hoping for something a bit more satisfying."

Aunt Jenny shrugged, and then she turned to Roberta, who'd been making sure everyone's drinks were topped off during the donut breakfast. "Bring out the cereal, please."

"No eggs and bacon?" Frank asked.

"Not this morning," Aunt Jenny said simply.

"Then I'll pass," Frank said as he grabbed a few glazed yeast donuts and scarfed them down.

"Anyone else unhappy with our breakfast buffet?" our hostess asked.

When no one else wanted cereal either, Aunt Jenny said, "Never mind, Roberta. If we're all finished, let's retire to the drawing room for this morning's activity."

As we walked out, I touched Aunt Jenny's arm lightly. "Were they really okay?"

"They were delightful," she said.

I wanted to ask her how she was feeling, but we weren't alone, and I didn't want to give any of the other guests any reason to be suspicious about our hostess's health. "I'm glad," I said.

Paige pulled me aside as everyone else moved into the drawing room. "Don't let Calvin bother you. He's that way with everybody."

"I'm not worried about Calvin," I said with a slight smile.

"That's my girl. You outdid yourself, Suzanne. Those donuts were amazing."

"Thank you."

"I hope you didn't mind making them. It meant a great deal to Aunt Jenny."

"It's not all that unusual for me to have to sing for my supper, but in this case, it was my honor," I told her.

"You're my kind of people, you know that, don't you?"

"I hope so," I told her, returning the squeeze of her hand that she'd just given me.

"Are you two coming?" Aunt Jenny asked. She'd paused at the door to wait on us. "Trust me, you don't want to miss out on today's prizes."

"We're right behind you," Paige said. "But you know you don't have to bribe us to come hang out with you. We'd happily do it for free."

"I couldn't have said it better myself," I added.

"Bless you both, but this is fun for me! Now, let's go."

We did as we were told, and there were a few covert looks in our direction as we walked in practically arm and arm with Aunt Jenny. I found myself wanting to win again, not for the prize but for the expressions it would surely create on those faces.

Chapter 9

"This morning's activity is a scavenger hunt," Aunt Jenny said. "For this one, you will work in teams of two, and as before, you have one hour to find as many objects on the list as you can. I'll draw the names randomly from this bowl for your pairings. When you find an item, take one, and only one, and leave the rest for your fellow contestants. You should be warned that Calvin and Roberta will be monitoring the contest randomly, and any cheaters will not only be disqualified from the hunt, but they will be escorted from the premises immediately, forfeiting all prizes won to that point. Do I make myself clear?"

She did, and though there were some sullen looks among the group members, everyone agreed to the rules.

"Excellent," Aunt Jenny said. "When you and your partner are chosen, go to one corner of the room to await your list of the items you'll be hunting for. The following rooms are off limits: all bedrooms, the kitchen, and my late husband's study."

"Does the search area extend outside, or is it all indoors?" Bess asked. It was a clever question, one I hadn't thought to ask.

"Did I mention outdoors as being out of bounds?" Aunt Jenny asked with a slight smile. "No? I wonder why. Are there any other questions? None at all? Honestly, Bess, I'm surprised you asked that in front of everyone else. You could have had quite the advantage over the others if you'd pulled me aside privately later."

Bess's face turned three shades of scarlet, which drew smirks from Frank and Sandy. Bess realized the magnitude of her blunder, but there was nothing she could do about it after the fact.

"Very well. Let's begin." Aunt Jenny reached into a large crystal punch bowl that was probably worth a small fortune and pulled out the first name.

"Bess," she said, crumpling the paper and putting it into her pocket. "And her partner is... Frank."

"Great," Frank said sarcastically.

"I'm not thrilled about it, either," Bess said.

"Come now. This is meant to be fun."

"What are we playing for, exactly?" Sandy asked.

"Where would the joy in my telling you that be?" Aunt Jenny asked. "Next up, we have Bobbi."

I found myself saying under my breath, "Please, not me. Don't call out my name," but nobody heard me.

Except for Paige, evidently.

She whispered, "Not me, either," and we both chuckled softly, though no one else knew what we were laughing about.

Aunt Jenny pulled out another name, looked me directly in the eye, and I felt my heart sink.

Then she said the name Sandy.

"That leaves Paige and Suzanne as our last pairing," Aunt Jenny said, smiling broadly. As she handed out the sheets with our needed items, everyone left the room at a dead run.

Except Paige.

"Mind if I check the last two names in the bowl?" she asked her honorary aunt with a smile.

Aunt Jenny reached in and plucked them out before she could, crumpling them all together. "There's no need."

"You didn't rig the contest in our favor, did you?" Paige asked her.

"Paige," I reprimanded her, though I'd been wondering the same thing myself.

"Well, did you?" Paige asked, ignoring me for the moment.

"You're wasting precious time, ladies," she said, holding that same level expression she'd had earlier. I would hate to play poker with this woman. She was too good at masking her emotions.

"Fine," Paige said, "but no cheating, Aunt Jenny. You said it yourself."

"What on earth makes you think that applies to me?" our hostess asked with a grin.

I had a sudden thought. "So I didn't really win last night after all? I can't accept the necklace then, no matter how gracious of you it was to give it to me."

"My dear, you won that contest fair and square. Now go. Trust me, you don't want to miss out on the prizes this round."

"Come on, Suzanne. Let's go," Paige said as she tugged at my arm.

I stood there a moment longer, but Aunt Jenny wasn't giving a thing away. "Fine. I'm right behind you," I told my game partner.

Once we were nearly out of the room, I glanced back at our hostess and saw her crumple more than sit on the sofa just behind her. I wanted to see if I could help her in any way, but Calvin was taking care of her in an instant as Roberta closed and locked the door between us.

I decided not to worry about the results the night before. I was too concerned about Aunt Jenny's health to care much about anything else at the moment. Still, she'd clearly wanted Paige and me to team up together, and if we could win, I knew that it would make her happy.

"What's a golden pinecone?" I asked Paige as I started reading the list we'd been given.

"Maybe from a golden pine?" she asked me.

"Would you know a golden pine from a bronze one?"

"Let's just hope there's only one kind of pine on the property," Paige said. "What else is on the list?"

I scanned the items and read them aloud as we walked around the property. I wasn't sure if it was a good sign or not, but none of the other teams were nearby. Either we were better off than the rest of them or worse. "Okay, here goes. Besides the golden pinecone, we're supposed to find a black marble, a yellow rose, ball of yarn, a golf ball, a ruler, a letter opener, and a white candle. We don't have much time, do we?"

"No, but no one else does, either. An hour isn't a lot. Maybe we should go see where everyone else is."

"Why be followers?" I asked Paige. "Look. Is that a cluster of golf balls under that tree?"

Sure enough, we found three golf balls, one for each team, under a Japanese maple near the back garden. "That's one," I said as I grabbed the closest one to us.

"Just seven more items left," Paige said. "Now, come on, let's go in the house."

"Fine, but I still think something else might be outside. Why don't we walk around the perimeter first?"

"Can we split up?" Paige asked me suddenly. "We'll cover twice the ground that way."

"We're playing as a team," I said uncertainly. "Doesn't that mean we have to stick together?"

"Aunt Jenny didn't say that we did," Paige said with a smile. "Good luck."

Before I could say another word, she was heading into the house.

Fine. We might lose, but I didn't *think* we were cheating. At least, I hoped Aunt Jenny didn't think so. I didn't care about the necklace—okay, that wasn't quite true—but I was more concerned about earning Aunt Jenny's disappointment than losing a fortune I didn't really feel all that entitled to anyway. I walked around the plantings in back, studied the pond and the birdbath, even investigated under the whimsical garden gnome, but I didn't find another item on our list.

In fact, I nearly missed the black marbles near the front door, clustered in one of the planters. There was one other marble there, so one other team had found one. Still, it had to be a good sign that we'd found ours.

I walked into the entryway to find that the other two teams had broken up as well. Evidently, if one of us was going to get kicked out, we all would. "What did you find?" Bess asked me as she tried to corner me before I could get past her.

I shoved the golf ball and the marble into my jeans pocket. "I'm sorry, I didn't realize the teams had changed again."

"They haven't," Bess said, "but you've already won something. Leave a thing or two for the rest of us, why don't you?"

"Paige hasn't won anything yet," I reminded her. "Your time might be better spent searching instead of trying to browbeat me into telling you anything."

"Fine, be that way," she said angrily before disappearing into a room I hadn't been in before. Bess was attractive, there was no doubt about it, but she was like a beautifully wrapped present with nothing but junk inside. In a way, I pitied her. After all, I'd been called cute at my best—never beautiful, if you didn't count Jake—and it had worked out just fine for me. Speaking of my husband, I thought about giving him a call, but it wouldn't be fair to Paige if I played hooky during one of her aunt's contests. Besides, knowing Jake, he was in it up to his eyebrows running the police department. I'd call him later that evening, but for now, it was time to resume my search.

I saw Paige a few times, but we just waved and kept hunting.

Unfortunately, by the time the gong sounded, I still had only two items. Paige was about to show me her stash when Calvin announced, "Come in one group at a time, in the order you were chosen. No more hunting, though," he said as he pointed toward Roberta. "She'll make sure of that."

"I'm sorry. I didn't do very well," I told Paige softly. "Besides the golf ball, I found a black marble."

"That's okay. I found enough for both of us," she answered as she showed me her loot. She'd snatched a yellow rose miniature, a tiny ball of yarn, a small white birthday candle, and a mini ruler.

"Between the two of us, we have everything except the letter opener and the pinecone," I told her. "How do you think the others did?"

"I have no idea, but we'll find out soon enough," she answered as Calvin came back in for the second team, leaving us alone with Aunt Jenny's assistant.

I decided to take a moment to ask Roberta a question. "How's Aunt Jenny doing?" I asked her.

"She's fine," the young woman said curtly.

"I saw what happened, and she didn't look fine to me at all," I pushed.

"What are you talking about, Suzanne?" Paige asked me.

"Aunt Jenny collapsed onto the couch as we left the room for the scavenger hunt," I explained.

"And you didn't say anything to me at the time *why*, exactly?" She seemed a bit upset with me, and I couldn't blame her.

"I didn't think there was anything we could do about it, and it was important to her that we do well," I answered. "If I messed up, I'm sorry."

Ignoring me, Paige asked Roberta, "Is she okay?"

"She felt a bit faint, but she's fine now. I promise," she answered. "Suzanne's right. She insisted that I lock the door and not let anyone in, so there was nothing you could have done for her. Calvin and I are perfectly capable of seeing to her needs. You know that."

"I'm sorry. She's just really important to me," Paige said.

"As you are to her," Roberta said softly.

"Do you forgive me?" I asked Paige.

"I get it," she answered, which was not really the question I'd asked her.

"Listen, if you think I didn't say anything because I'm concerned about prizes, take the necklace. I don't want it."

"No, I don't think that. I'm sorry, Suzanne. This party has me on edge, but there's no reason for me to take it out on you."

"Hey, if you'll stop apologizing to me, I'll stop doing it to you," I told her. "Is it a deal?"

"It is," she said as she tried to hug me. We both heard something snap, and she pulled out the candle, which was now in two pieces but still connected by the wick. "I hope that still counts."

"It had better," I told her as Calvin called us inside.

"Ladies," he said, nodding to me as I walked past him.

"Gentleman," I said just as solemnly.

He had to bite his lip not to smile, so I considered that a point in my favor.

Once we showed Aunt Jenny our stash, there was a celebration from Bess and Frank. "We won!" she shouted, celebrating their victory. "Good job," she added in a softer voice to Frank.

"You too," Frank said as he turned expectantly to Aunt Jenny. "What exactly did we win?"

"We'll get to that in a moment," our hostess said as she looked at the four of us who hadn't won. "I knew the letter openers would be difficult to find, and none of you did, but why were the golden pinecones difficult for two of the teams? They were on the back terrace, floating on a small boat in the pond. I never dreamed just one team would find them."

"There wasn't anything in the pond," I told her. "I looked."

"Hey, just because everyone else missed them doesn't mean that they weren't there," Bess protested. "After all, *we* found one."

"Let's go out and see, shall we?" Aunt Jenny asked.

"We won, fair and square," Frank stated.

"We shall see," our hostess replied.

They both looked troubled by this development, but I wanted to see that pond again as well. Something was fishy, and I didn't mean the koi swimming around in it.

Just as I suspected, there was no boat in sight. "See?" I asked.

Aunt Jenny peered closer at the water and saw something on the bottom. "It appears the boat sank."

"Or was sunk on purpose," Sandy said. I was surprised to hear the meek woman protest, but who knew what kind of prize was at stake?

"It doesn't matter how it happened," Bess said. "We took just one golden pinecone. You can see the other two down there. We abided by the letter of the law."

"If not the spirit," Aunt Jenny said.

"Does that mean you're going to cheat us out of our prizes?" the bantam man complained. "We followed your blasted rules."

"In a way, I suppose you did," Aunt Jenny said with a frown. "Very well. We have our winners." She then turned to us. "I'm sorry, folks."

"It's fine," Paige said.

"Maybe with you," Bobbi answered under her breath. I was standing close enough to hear it, but I doubted that anyone else had.

"Your prizes are out front," Aunt Jenny said. "The keys are in the ignitions."

We all went out to see what the dirty players had won. There was a pair of matching blue Jeep Gladiators in the driveway, each sporting its own large red ribbon.

"She gets a necklace worth a fortune and we get *these*?" Bess asked, the outrage heavy in her voice. "Why did you even have these?"

"Gray thought they'd be fun, but we never had the chance to drive them. Go look inside," Aunt Jenny told them, refusing to rise to the bait.

Bess raced to the closest car and threw the door open. In a moment, she held something aloft in triumph. "It's a Rolex watch, but it's for a man."

"Then the other automobile is yours," Aunt Jenny said.

The two traded off, and Bess pulled out the woman's watch and immediately put it on. "It still isn't worth what Suzanne won last night."

"Guess again," Aunt Jenny said. "The watch is worth twenty thousand dollars, and the Jeep is worth fifty thousand."

"That's just seventy, and hers is worth a hundred grand," Frank protested.

"Together, your prizes are worth more," she answered. "If you're unhappy with what you've won, I'm sure one of the others would be more than happy to take your prizes off your hands."

"Absolutely," Bobbi said, while the rest of us nodded.

No surprise, there were no offers. "No, it's fine. That will work," Bess said a bit glumly.

"I'm not giving mine up, so don't even bother asking," Frank added.

"You could thank Aunt Jenny for her generosity, you know," Paige said, getting in Bess's face.

"I figured that was implied," Bess answered, not backing down an inch.

"Say it," Paige repeated angrily. "Say thank you."

I put a hand on my friend's shoulder and pulled her away. "Do you honestly think it would be sincere at this point? Come on, let's go back inside."

"An excellent idea," Aunt Jenny said, dismissing the sore winners in an instant. "You have some free time until lunch, so feel free to walk the grounds."

"I want to take a nap," Sandy said. "I got up way too early."

"That's fine too," Aunt Jenny said.

"Do you have a second?" Paige asked her.

"It's not going to do you any good to complain," Bess said. "We won."

"It's not about that," Paige answered, not even looking back at the woman. "Aunt Jenny?"

She took her honorary niece's hands in hers and asked, "Can it wait? I have some things I really must take care of."

"Sure. Of course," she said.

After our hostess was gone, I saw that Paige was heading back toward Bess and Frank, who were complaining about their prizes.

"Let's go fish out those pinecones," I told her. "I want to see if they're really gold."

"I saw the one they had. It was spray-painted," Paige told me.

"Maybe not all of them were, though," I insisted, and she finally gave in and joined me.

"Are we *really* going to try to pull those things out of the water?"

"Not unless you want to," I said. "I was just trying to give you a chance to cool off before you did something you shouldn't have."

"I can't believe those two cheated like that," Paige replied.

"I don't like it any more than you do, but Aunt Jenny said that we couldn't take more than one of each item, and they didn't do that. They just found a loophole in her rule."

"Are you saying you *approve* of what they did, sinking that boat so none of the rest of us would find it?" Paige asked me, clearly disturbed by the thought.

"Not a chance, but I don't know why you are so surprised."

"I'm not. I continually find myself disappointed with *most* people's behavior *most* of the time."

"Again, we agree," I said. "Now, let's put that behind us and take a walk out to the bridge."

"Why?" she asked.

"It beats going inside and spending more time with Bess, Frank, Sandy, and Bobbi, doesn't it?"

"You've got a point," Paige said as she smiled. "Suzanne, have you tried using your cell phone since we got here?"

"No, I was going to call Jake after lunch," I told her.

"Good luck with that. I tried to check my messages this morning, and I couldn't get a signal. That's mountain life, I guess."

"Is there a landline at the house? I'd really like to talk to my husband," I told her.

"Sure, Aunt Jenny has one in her room. I'm sure she'd let you use it."

"Excellent," I said. "Now, let's take that walk."

It was shorter than I thought it was going to be, though.

The bridge, at least where it had been the day before, was now gone, taken out by a tree that must have fallen during the storm we'd had the night before.

It was then that I noticed the cell phone tower I'd spotted on the drive in was missing as well.

No wonder we hadn't been able to get signals on our phones.

We were isolated, trapped until someone realized that we were there, cut off from the rest of the world.

Chapter 10

We hurried back to the house and found Aunt Jenny in a private conversation with Calvin in the kitchen. Fortunately, no one else was around.

"The bridge is out, and the cell phone tower's down too," Paige said, huffing from the rapid pace of our return.

"We know," Aunt Jenny said softly. "Keep your voices down, please. Calvin discovered it just before the scavenger hunt, and we've been discussing what we should do."

"Is your landline working?" I asked her. "Maybe we could get someone out here that way."

"Unfortunately, the telephone line ran directly under the bridge," Aunt Jenny said.

"So we're trapped here?" Paige asked dramatically.

"I suppose that's one way to look at it," Aunt Jenny said, being much calmer at the moment than I was being.

"What does it *really* mean, though?" Calvin asked. "We have plenty of food, our power is still on, and we're not in any danger at all. With any luck, we'll get the bridge fixed before anyone else knows what's going on."

"How are they supposed to even know we're cut off here?" I asked him.

Aunt Jenny answered for him. "After lunch, Calvin is going to cross the gulley and hike to my nearest neighbor. I'm not without influence, so I'm sure something will be done to allow us all to leave as soon as possible."

"You really aren't worried a bit, are you?" I asked her, admiring her calm.

"Suzanne, with the things I've experienced in my life, this doesn't even make the top ten times I've been in a jam. From what I gather from my research on the Internet, you could say the same thing yourself."

"I've been up against it a time or two," I admitted.

"Or three," Paige added with a smile. "Okay. Sorry we panicked."

"You did the right thing coming to me first. You *did* come to me first, didn't you? You didn't happen to tell anyone else what you found, did you?"

"No, ma'am. Are we keeping this a secret?" Paige asked her.

"Let me ask you this. What good would it do the others to find out they can't leave at any time? Would *you* like to deal with that?"

"Not a chance," Paige answered. "So it's business as usual then."

"I believe that's our best course of action. We'll have lunch, and then Calvin will go for help. With any luck, he won't be missed before he gets back. I suspect he won't. I have a full set of puzzles ready for you all this afternoon."

"Are you really going on with the gift party?" I asked her. "From the way Bess and Frank acted, nobody would blame you for ending your contests right now."

"I'm not about to let those two spoil our fun," Aunt Jenny said. "Don't worry. This afternoon's contest will be a bit more supervised than the last one was."

"Care to give us any hints about what we'll be doing?" Paige asked her with a grin.

Smiling just as broadly, Aunt Jenny said, "No, not particularly."

"You don't mind me asking, though, right?"

"I would have been disappointed if one of you hadn't," our hostess answered with a smile.

"Do you need me to put lunch out so Calvin can get started early?" I offered.

"Suzanne, don't you think you've put in enough work in this weekend?" Aunt Jenny asked me.

"I don't mind pitching in," she said.

Calvin smiled at me, and he didn't even seem to care that Paige caught it as well. "Thanks, partner, but I've got this. If I need you, though, I'll holler."

"You'd better," I said.

"Let's have an early lunch, shall we?" Aunt Jenny asked. "I'd like Calvin back before dark."

"You don't think anything is going to happen, do you?" I asked her. I'd interviewed too many witnesses not to know uneasiness when I heard it in someone's voice.

"No, I just feel it will be safer if he doesn't have to traipse around the woods in the dark," Aunt Jenny said. "Go get everyone together and announce lunch. I'm afraid it's going to be cold cuts and fruit today. Oh, I can't wait to hear the grumbling." She looked almost delighted by the prospect of her guests complaining.

"You really are enjoying this, aren't you?" I asked her.

"More than you can know," Aunt Jenny replied. "Now, go, ladies. We have a busy schedule ahead of us."

Just as our hostess had predicted, there were numerous complaints about the food being offered for lunch, and it was all I could do not to smile. In fact, something must have slipped for just a moment.

"Is there something about this meal that amuses you, Suzanne?" Frank asked me pointedly.

"No. As a matter of fact, I think it's delicious," I said. "This bread is homemade, isn't it? I can see sesame seeds, pumpkin seeds, and is that flax I'm tasting?"

"It is," Calvin said. "I made it myself yesterday."

"I'd love to have the recipe," I said. "It's amazing."

"You've got it," Calvin said.

Paige looked back and forth between the chef and me, but she didn't say anything. I'd have to tell her that Calvin wasn't nearly as bad as he pretended to be. I'd hold back the secret about Aunt Jenny's health, but if I tried to keep *every* secret I knew, I'd probably explode.

For dessert, Calvin had whipped up a chocolate cake that had to have been made from scratch. I didn't know why others were complaining. I didn't eat this well at home, and I suspected they didn't, either.

"Now that we're finished with lunch, let's go to the ballroom. Roberta has set things up for our next series of challenges," Aunt Jenny said. "Calvin, you've been working hard since very early this morning. Why don't you take the afternoon off?"

That was clever. If anyone noticed Calvin's absence when he went for help, Aunt Jenny had explained it beforehand.

"Thanks. I could use a nap," he said as he started clearing away the dishes. I started to help, more out of habit than anything else, when Aunt Jenny said, "Suzanne, the games are about to begin, and trust me, you don't want to miss out on this prize."

"What is it?" Bess asked. "Care to at least share with us what we're playing for this afternoon?"

"I do not," Aunt Jenny replied without any of the warmth she'd used denying Paige's earlier request.

"Hey, you can't blame a gal for trying," Bess said under her breath.

"I'm sorry. What was that?" Aunt Jenny asked.

"I said 'fair enough,'" she lied.

I thought about correcting her, but honestly, it wasn't worth the grief.

We all followed Aunt Jenny into the ballroom, where six tables had been set up as far away from each other as possible. There were six matching chairs, but the tabletops themselves were bare.

"Would everyone please take a seat," she instructed.

I did as I was told, and as I did, I realized that it was impossible to see any of the other tables from where I sat without being noticed. There wouldn't be any cheating this afternoon; that was for sure.

"Roberta, please hand out the booklets," Aunt Jenny said as she placed three sharpened number-two pencils at each desk.

"Don't open your booklets until I tell you to," Aunt Jenny said.

Once we all had them in front of us, I looked at mine. It sported a plain blue cover, and there was a white circle of paper band sealing it shut. There was no way to open the booklet without tearing that seal, at least not without one of the letter openers we'd all been unsuccessful at finding for the earlier scavenger hunt.

"You will have two hours to solve as many of the puzzles presented as possible. There will be no talking, no standing, no leaving your seat until the allotted time is up."

"What if we need to sharpen one of our pencils?" Bobbi asked. "I always press too hard and break the lead."

"Try your best not to," Aunt Jenny said. "Roberta will be monitoring you the entire time, and I'll be sitting over there, watching as well," she said as she gestured to a comfortable armchair that gave her a clear sightline to each of us. "Are there any questions?"

"May we take a bathroom break before we get started?" Sandy asked.

"Of course. Actually, that's not a bad idea."

Frank started to get up too.

"Leave the booklet at your table, Frank," Roberta told him sternly.

"This? I forgot I was still holding it," he said, which was clearly a lie.

After everyone who needed a break took one, Aunt Jenny turned on the large clock that had timed us the night before. "You have two hours, beginning right now," she said as she flipped a switch.

We all ripped open the booklets and dug in, and I couldn't help wondering what kind of tests I was about to take.

To my surprise, they were mostly all ones I'd seen before. There were loads of scrambled-letter puzzles, crossword puzzles, number puzzles, word problems, and finally, a small box containing two different jigsaw puzzles were handed out as we read the instructions to our challenge. I couldn't see if those puzzles were all the same with the other participants, but mine featured a small pizza, and the other sported a small sprinkled donut.

At least that part of the challenge would be right up my alley!

I decided to tackle things in order. I had always been a whiz at unscrambling letters in any type of puzzle, so those didn't offer much resistance. The crosswords had a few clues I didn't know, and I had to leave six spaces blank on one and three on the other, but time was racing past quickly, so I needed to move on. If I had the chance I'd go back and see if I could figure them out, but they would have to wait for now.

The number puzzles I skipped completely. I'd never gotten the hang of sudoku, Ken Ken, or any of the other popular number puzzles. My mind just didn't seem to work that way. Again, if I had time, I'd go back and tackle them, but they were a low priority for me at the moment. The word problems were trick questions, and I answered them fairly simply, but time was running out. I had seven minutes left to solve two jigsaw puzzles. Fortunately, I liked doing them, and the pizza puzzle went together quickly. I couldn't believe that the donut puzzle, of all things, was tripping me up the most! The edges of it were round, and I had a hard time wrapping my head around the odd shape. I glanced at the clock and saw that I had less than a minute left, so in a move of desperation, I started putting sections together that matched and not worry about the overall puzzle. That was clearly the secret as I placed the last piece, the hole no less, as time expired.

"Pencils down NOW," Roberta said as she collected our writing instruments from us.

"Leave your places and go to the lounge area. We'll be out soon with the results," Aunt Jenny said.

I saw Frank try to make one last move toward the pizza puzzle, but before I could say anything, Aunt Jenny added, "I said NOW!"

We left the room while the results were tabulated. I felt bad about leaving the number puzzles blank, but honestly, there was no way I would have been able to finish everything in the allotted time. I'd just have to hope that the others had their own areas of weakness. I found that I wanted to win, not because of the promised riches at the end but for the sheer sake of winning.

"How'd you do?" Paige asked me.

"There's no talking," Bess snapped.

"No one said anything about being quiet this time," I corrected her. I pulled Paige away from the others. "I had to skip a few puzzles altogether, and I left a few other answers blank. How about you?"

"Those scrambled-letter puzzles drove me crazy! I got the answers, but it took way too long."

"How about the number puzzles?" I asked her.

"Piece of cake. I flew through the crossword puzzles and the word problems too, and I've been doing jigsaw puzzles since I was a little girl. In fact, that was one of the things I did the most with Aunt Jenny. She loves them."

"So do I," I said. It sounded as though Paige had filled in more answers than I had, but if she won, I'd have no problem with it. In fact, it would be a crime if she left the weekend without anything.

After all, she had the longest and certainly the most caring relationship with Aunt Jenny.

Tabulating the results seemed to take forever, but our hostess finally came out, with Roberta trailing close behind her. "You all did well, but two of you frankly surprised me. There were two winners, a deadlock that I refuse to settle with a tiebreaker. Thus, I will award equal prizes to the two winners, Sandy and Bobbi."

"I *won*?" Bobbi asked, clearly incredulous. "Honestly, I had to guess on a few of my answers."

"*We* won," Sandy corrected her. "And I didn't guess at all." She seemed a bit chagrined that she'd be sharing the prize with anyone else, though Aunt Jenny had clearly told us that the prizes would be the same.

"What do they get?" Bess asked sarcastically. "More vehicles that nobody wants to drive?"

Aunt Jenny ignored her. "Actually, I'm awarding them each stock worth a hundred thousand dollars each," she said.

"Come on," Frank protested. "That's hardly fair. We got vehicles and watches, but they get stock? Can we trade?"

"You may not," Aunt Jenny said. Turning to the two women, she said, "The stocks will be signed over to you Monday morning. Congratulations."

"Is that when we'll get the titles to our vehicles?" Bess asked.

"It is." Aunt Jenny frowned for a moment, and then she said, "In fact, I don't think it's fair for *anyone* to get their prizes until we've finished with the weekend's festivities. Bess, Frank, I'll thank you both to return the keys to your Gladiators to me, as well as the watches."

"I'll go grab the necklace," I volunteered without being asked.

"Thank you," Aunt Jenny said.

"I'm happy to do it," I said. "I'll be right back."

Only I wasn't.

I was still in our room when Paige came in. "Suzanne, everyone's waiting for you. Grab the necklace and come back."

"That's the thing," I said as I pointed to the jewelry box, nearly ready to cry. "It's gone."

Chapter 11

"What do you mean, it's gone? Are you sure?" Paige asked me in disbelief.

"Trust me, I've been tearing this place apart, looking for it ever since I saw that the box was empty. You didn't get it out this morning and try it on again, by any chance, did you? I'm not mad. I'm only asking."

"I didn't touch it," she said.

"Well, I didn't, either. What am I going to tell Aunt Jenny?"

"The truth," she said. "Someone came into our room and stole your necklace. How did they think they would possibly get away with it? We're isolated here, so there's no way to smuggle it out."

"That's the thing, though. No one else knows that the bridge is gone," I told her. "They could have stolen it thinking they could make a quick getaway. This is going to break Aunt Jenny's heart."

"Or make her cancel the entire weekend," Paige said.

"Would that be such a bad thing?" I asked her as we finally realized there was no point in continuing our search.

"I told her to call it off last week, but she wouldn't listen to me. I don't care about her stuff. All that matters to me is that I have her around."

I wanted to respect our hostess's wishes, but I couldn't bring myself to do it. Not anymore. "Paige, there's something you should know."

"That Aunt Jenny's dying?" she asked me softly.

"You already knew?"

"I did. Before you get upset with me, I knew she was keeping it a secret, so I didn't feel right sharing it with you," Paige said softly.

"She made me promise not to tell you too," I said. "Forgive me?"

"We're good, Suzanne. I'm glad you said something, though. I don't want there to be any secrets between us."

I blurted out, "I have one more. Calvin's really a nice guy. He's not nearly the jerk he pretends to be."

"Feel better?" Paige asked me with a grin.

"I really do. He asked me not to tell anyone. How long have you known I felt that way?"

"Ever since I saw your change of attitude toward him this morning," she admitted. "Don't worry, his secret is safe with me too. I still think he's a jerk, but I'm happy you don't."

"I feel terrible about losing the necklace, but I'm glad there aren't any other secrets between us."

"You didn't *lose* it, Suzanne. Someone stole it, and the sooner we tell Aunt Jenny, the better. Come on. It's going to be okay."

"I don't see how, but I agree it's better to get it over with."

"What? Are you certain?" Aunt Jenny asked me after we told her the news. "It hasn't just been mislaid?"

"It's gone," I said flatly.

"We both tore up the room looking for it," Paige added, backing me up.

"This is ridiculous," Frank said. "No one stole your precious necklace. You simply didn't find it and jumped to a false conclusion."

"I never said it was stolen," I told him coldly. "In fact, I went to great pains *not* to say that."

"Well, it was implied, and I, for one, don't appreciate anyone thinking that I had anything to do with it," Frank said.

"Well, I certainly didn't take it," Bess chimed in.

"I didn't, either," Sandy added.

"I didn't do it," Bobbi finished.

"We have no choice, ladies," Aunt Jenny said. "I hate to invade your privacy, but I need to look for myself."

"Be our guest," I told her.

"We're coming too," Bess said, and the others nodded in agreement.

"Fine. I don't care who comes along," I told them. "At this point, we have nothing to hide."

"We'll just see about that," Bess said archly. What did she mean by that?

It didn't matter how many people searched. Even after tearing the sheets off, pulling every towel out of the bathroom, and riffling through our luggage, the necklace was still missing by the time we were finished demolishing our room. Aunt Jenny had supervised the search from one of the chairs, but only after searching the cushions for the necklace in case it had slipped down between them.

"There's no other conclusion. The necklace has been stolen," she said solemnly.

"I'm not going to put up with being accused of theft," Frank said. "Give me the keys to my Jeep, and I'm leaving."

"It isn't your Jeep," Paige reminded him. "At least, not yet."

"Then I'll take the junk car I came in."

"No, you won't," Aunt Jenny said firmly.

"This is garbage," Bess protested. "Were you ever intending to award us any of these prizes?"

"I was going to do exactly that until someone stole one of them," Aunt Jenny said. Before more protests could erupt, she added, "Nothing's been decided, but we need to find that necklace, and I mean now."

"What do you propose?" Sandy asked.

"We search the house from top to bottom," our hostess said gravely.

"Including our rooms?" Bobbi asked, clearly unhappy about the prospect of what had happened here occurring in her space.

"We have no choice," Aunt Jenny said.

It didn't do us any good, though.

Whoever had taken my necklace had done a superior job hiding it. For all intents and purposes, it was gone.

"What about the help?" Frank asked after we'd searched everywhere else. "It makes sense that one of your servants saw an opportunity to steal a valuable piece of jewelry and took it."

"That is ridiculous," Aunt Jenny said. "I'd trust them both with my life."

"Good for you," Bess said, "but if you're going to subject us to this indignity, they deserve no less."

She had a point, but I wasn't about to back her up, especially since I knew Calvin wasn't resting in his room, as everyone else assumed. How would the crowd react if they knew we were cut off from the rest of the world here? I wasn't sure, but I had a feeling it wouldn't be pretty.

Bobbi was the one who pointed out the obvious. "Calvin's probably still napping, so we can't go in there."

"We'll wake him," Bess said. "Boo hoo. He can go back to sleep after we're finished, but I'm not about to let my name be dragged through the mud like this. I won't have anyone suspect me of stealing when I didn't do it."

Did that mean she didn't mind being a suspect if she'd actually *committed* the theft? It was a rather telling statement, but I decided not to call her on it. After all, there was enough tension in the group without me adding fuel to the fire.

"I'm afraid we have no choice," Aunt Jenny said as she looked at us for help.

Paige came up with a solution before I could. "I thought I saw him walking by the pond when I went to help Suzanne look, so he may not even be in his room."

"I saw him, too, now that you mention it," I said, backing her up.

"There you go. We'll search his room before he gets back." Aunt Jenny had told the literal truth, since Calvin was indeed gone, but farther from us than anyone else imagined.

His room, small and Spartan, was neat as a pin, though not after we finished tearing it up. I made an effort to straighten things back up when Bess laughed. "Leave it for him. We have bigger fish to fry."

I shrugged, torn between my desire to make things right there and to keep searching with the rest of the group.

I'm afraid the latter part of me won.

Roberta, much to my surprise, was an absolute pig when it came to her room. Clothes were strewn everywhere, and things were piled up on the dresser in what could only be described as chaos. I had a hard time matching what we found with what I'd seen of the assistant so far.

There was no necklace anywhere, though.

"That just leaves your room," Sandy said as she looked at Aunt Jenny.

Our hostess looked genuinely surprised by the thought of it. "Why would I steal something I was clearly so ready to give away?"

"What if you had a change of heart?" Frank said. "She's got a point. That is, if you truly do want to be fair."

"That is outrageous," I said, springing to Aunt Jenny's defense. "You've all clearly lost your minds."

"It's fine, Suzanne," my new friend said. "They are right. It's only fair."

We looked through Aunt Jenny's space, albeit much more delicately than we had the other rooms, and to no one's surprise, there was no evidence of the necklace.

"This doesn't prove anything," Bess said once we were reassembled in the ballroom. "It just means that whoever hid it knew what they were doing."

"What now?" Bobbi asked.

"I need to think," Aunt Jenny said. "If you'll all excuse me, I wish to put my room back in order, and I suggest you all do the same."

"We can give you a hand," Paige said, but our hostess merely shook her head, and we all decided to give her some space. I was sure that it hadn't been easy on any of us having our privacy disrupted, but for Aunt Jenny, it was the ultimate insult. After all, she'd gathered us together to give away some of her wealth, not cause so much animosity between us all. It was like I'd been known to say on occasion: "No good deed goes unpunished." I never used to think that way, but experience had a way of taking the shine off things for me. It was no doubt at least partly because I had spent so much of my time investigating murders and seeing the darker side of things, but maybe I could get a bit of the joy back once I stopped digging into the darkness within so many people. I hoped so. I certainly didn't want this to be how I ended up, expecting the worst out of people and usually getting it.

Once we were back in our room, I said, "I hate that this happened. It's absolutely crushed Aunt Jenny."

"I know that she was feeling bad before, but I'm afraid what this is going to do to her," Paige said as she continued to straighten things up. "Suzanne, do you have *any* idea who took your necklace?"

"What makes you think I know more about it than anyone else does?" I asked her as I tried to get everything back into my suitcase. No matter how well I packed at home for a trip, I always seemed to magically end up with more than I'd brought, even when I hadn't added anything to my possessions.

"Come on. You're a sleuth, remember?" she asked.

"An amateur one at best," I corrected her.

"You've solved more cases than a lot of cops have. Who do you think did it?"

"Paige! I don't have any evidence one way or the other," I said hotly as I remade my bed, hoping against all hope that we'd all somehow missed it and it would magically reappear.

It didn't.

My friend's tone was conciliatory as she said, "Hey, it's me, remember? I'm not interviewing you for the newspaper or interrogating you as a cop. I'm just curious. Come on, play along."

I nodded. "I'm so sorry. I'm a bit out of sorts. I didn't mean to snap at you."

"You get a free pass, Suzanne. After all, I don't know if you've noticed, but I'm the *only* guest here who hasn't won anything. I'm the one who has a reason to be testy."

"I'm sure you will win something soon," I told her, suddenly feeling bad for my friend.

"Honestly, I couldn't care less. Like I said before, I'd be here so I could see Aunt Jenny, no matter what. Frankly, none of the rest of this matters to me."

"You mean that, don't you?" I asked as I looked into her eyes.

"You'd better believe it, and you feel the same way, so don't try to tell me otherwise. I've seen you bond with her so fast that I'm a little bit jealous myself. What is with you two?"

"What can I say? We're kindred spirits," I allowed, "but she loves you like a daughter, Paige. It's obvious enough every time she looks at you."

My friend smiled a bit. "I feel the same way about her. I can't believe she's dying."

"I know. It's a tough pill to swallow." I decided to lighten the mood between us, even if it meant putting what I knew so far to the test. "Okay, here are my observations so far. Remember, this is all just idle speculation. I have absolutely nothing to go on but my instincts."

"I'd put your gut feeling against just about any cop's," she said.

"Including Jake's?" I asked.

"He's good at digging into the heart of the truth, but I've never seen anyone who could read people like you do, Suzanne. I bet you'd be one crazy good poker player."

"I don't know about that. I have trouble remembering if a full house beats a flush," I told her.

"It does. Every time," Paige answered promptly.

"Wow, who's the card sharp now?" I asked her with a grin.

"I've played a hand or two in my life," she admitted, "but we're getting off of the topic at hand."

"Fine. Here goes nothing, for what it's worth. Bess or Frank could have done it, though they are both too obvious in a way."

"What do you mean?"

"Let me ask you this way. If you had to guess, who would be at the top of your list?" I asked her.

"Bess or Frank," she admitted.

"Don't you think they know that? I would expect them to do something a bit more subtle than an outright theft, though they might assume that we'd discount them both as being too obvious."

"That's a rabbit hole I don't want to go down," Paige said. "Does that mean you think it was either Bobbi or Sandy?"

"I didn't say that," I allowed. "Still, Bobbi seems to have led a hard life, and when she found out she was getting a hundred grand in stocks, she almost exploded with joy. I have a feeling she's got some financial difficulties we don't know about."

"She does," Paige said simply.

"Have you been holding out on me?" I asked my roommate for the weekend.

"No. Yes. Maybe," she said.

"Wow, at least you've covered all of the bases."

"Unlike you, this isn't the first time I've met these people," she reminded me. "Besides, Aunt Jenny's talked about them over the years, and I've managed to pick a few things up along the way."

"I'd love to hear what you know," I told her as I settled into the chair Aunt Jenny had so recently vacated.

"Bobbi went through a bad divorce a few years ago, and I mean bad. Aunt Jenny warned her about the man, but she wouldn't listen, even when she showed her photos of him cheating on her a week before the wedding. He took just about everything she had, and she just let him. Aunt Jenny's been helping her out a bit, but not enough to support her. She wants her to learn to stand on her own two feet."

"Interesting. Does she resent Aunt Jenny for it?"

"Oh, yes, and so does Sandy."

"What's her story?"

"She invested everything she had, including a nice inheritance from her folks, in what turned out to be a scam. Aunt Jenny knew her parents, so she felt obligated to help her, but Sandy seems to expect more than that. Both she and Bobbi look at my aunt's wealth as something they are entitled to. A point of interest is that Sandy won the grand prize last year, a pair of earrings worth over eighty grand, but she sold them the second she got back to Charlotte, where she lives. Evidently, the money was gone in less than two weeks. She's simply bad with her finances, which proved Aunt Jenny's reluctance to buy either one of them out of the trouble they'd gotten themselves into."

"Wow, so that explains why they're both here," I said. "How about Frank and Bess?"

"Those two are a real pair," Paige said. "Frank is the son of Uncle Gray's college roommate, and evidently, there was a bond between them that Aunt Jenny can't explain to this day. She thinks Frank's dad got Uncle Gray out of a jam once, but she could never learn the truth. Gray once made her promise to give him the benefit of the doubt and include him in her life, and she's respected his wishes no matter how odious the man might be."

"So that leaves Bess," I said.

"I haven't figured that one out myself," Paige admitted. "There's a story there, but Aunt Jenny hasn't shared it with me, at least so far."

"Fine. We'll both try to figure it out," I said.

"We should talk about Calvin and Roberta," Paige said. "I have my own problems with each of them, but say what you will, they are devoted to Aunt Jenny. There's no way either one of them would steal your necklace, at least not while Aunt Jenny is still alive."

"You seem pretty sure about that," I told her as I ironed out a few wrinkles on the bedspread with my hands.

"I am," she answered. "No, it's one of the four other guests, if you ask me."

"But which one?" I asked. "That's the question."

"Well, we're not going to solve this sitting around in here, isolated from the rest of them," Paige said as she headed for the door. "I wonder if Calvin's made it back yet."

"I doubt it," I said. "He's taking on a challenging task, going for help. I'm not exactly sure what he's going to be able to do once he gets in touch with the rest of the world. Bridges aren't rebuilt overnight, you know."

"Don't kid yourself. My aunt has connections you wouldn't believe. If she wants to, she can hire the Army Corps of Engineers to get us out of here tomorrow."

"I don't think you can hire that bunch," I told her with a grin.

"You know what I mean," Paige said as she chuckled. "Come on. Let's go see what everyone else is up to."

"Do we have to?" I asked her. I couldn't believe someone had violated our privacy and robbed me of something I'd just gotten. I hated the idea of the trespassing nearly as much as I did the actual theft.

"We do," she said. "Come on, put on your sleuthing hat, and let's get going."

'Yes, ma'am," I told her. I wasn't sure how far I could push the others, but I'd try my best. I owed it to our hostess.

Chapter 12

"I was just about to come get you both," Aunt Jenny said as Paige and I walked into the lounge area.

"What's up? Is Calvin back?" I asked softly.

"No, and I'm a bit worried. Do you two mind making dinner? I'm not sure what he had planned, but surely there's something you can prepare. I've never been all that handy in the kitchen, and Suzanne, you did a remarkable job with breakfast. I hate to ask, but we have to feed them *something*."

"I don't think anyone wants more donuts this evening," I said.

"Don't be so modest. I've had your cooking before," Paige said. "I'm sure you can whip something good up."

"Well, I can't touch Momma's cooking, not to mention Angelica DeAngelis's," I told them, "but I suppose I can make a meal with that fantastic pantry of yours."

"That's the spirit. Let's do this. We can come up with something. We both know that I can barely boil water, but if you need something cut up, chopped, diced, or peeled, I'm your gal."

"Okay, let's go see what we can come up with," I said as I headed back toward the kitchen.

"You are a lifesaver, Suzanne," Aunt Jenny said.

"You might want to wait until you've had my cooking before you say that," I told her with a grin.

"I'm sure it will be delightful."

I decided to leave it at that. At least the pantry was well stocked.

"Okay, let's see what we've got," I said as I opened the large refrigerator. "Oh, good. Chicken breasts are thawed and ready to cook. I can do something with those. Paige, grab that big stockpot, go into the pantry, and fetch two large cans of chicken broth, and then start chopping mushrooms. They need to be sliced around a quarter inch thin."

"I'm on it, Chef," she said as she saluted me.

"Please, real chefs all over the world are rolling over in their graves when you call me that."

"Even the ones who aren't dead yet?" she asked me with a grin.

"No, those are rolling their eyes so far back into their heads that they can barely see sunlight," I told her.

I grabbed the olive oil and a large skillet. The chicken breasts were massive, so I took one of Calvin's ultra-sharp knives and cut them into more manageable chunks. After adding a bit of butter and some diced garlic to the pan, I turned the burner on medium-high heat. I dredged the chunks of chicken in the flour that I'd seasoned with some salt, pepper, and garlic powder. After shaking the loose flour free, I put the pieces in the skillet and cooked them a few minutes each on all sides. They wouldn't be all the way done, but I wanted a sear on them, and their time in the stockpot would take care of the rest.

Once the chicken pieces were well browned, I set them aside, put more butter in the pan, splashed in some chicken stock, and then added the mushrooms, stirring them constantly.

"Wow, you aren't afraid of butter, are you?" Paige asked me as she looked over my shoulder.

"Do you want it to be healthy or to taste good?" I asked her. "I can do both, but not without my recipe book. This should be fine for tonight."

"I'm not judging," she said. "It smells amazing."

"Thanks."

After the mushrooms were cooked a bit, I added more stock and released the fond on the bottom of the pan. The tiny brown chunks didn't look like much, but they had a world of flavor in them, and I planned on getting every bit of it. Once it was all released, I removed the mushrooms and poured more broth into the pan, leaving enough room for the cream that was to come. "You thought that was high-caloric cooking? Wait until you get a load of this," I asked as I added a substantial amount of cream to the liquid already there. Stirring it all together, I then removed it from the pan and put it all into the stockpot. Setting it to simmer, I tossed in the mostly cooked chicken chunks and gave it a good stir. After that, I took some of the dried pasta from the pantry, boiled some water, and cooked that as well.

"Is that it?" Paige asked.

"That depends. Would you like a hearty stew with some of Calvin's bread that's left over, or should we bake some potatoes in the microwave and eat some frozen veggies too?" I nuked two bags of veggies, and then I turned to Paige. "Your call."

"Make it a stew," she said. "That's easier, right?"

"At this point, it's all pretty simple."

"Stew it is, then," she repeated.

"Cool," I replied as I dumped the veggies into the pot, stirring everything up again. "That's simpler. I swear, if anyone complains, they can make something for themselves."

"If you tell them that beforehand, I'm willing to bet they'll all love whatever you serve," Paige said. "When will it be done?"

After I drained the pasta and added it to the pot, I grinned at her. "In five, four, three, two, and one, there you go," I said as I turned off the burner.

"Seriously? That was quick."

"Meals like this have gotten me out of time jams in the past," I told her as I grabbed a pair of oven mitts and pulled the pot off the massive gas stove. I knew that the meal wasn't up to Calvin's standards, but it should do. I tasted a spoonful, added a bit more salt and pepper, and then I offered a bite to Paige. "Thoughts?"

"Wow, that's really good," she said.

"Hey, try not to sound so surprised next time," I told her. "Now, let's slice the bread and toast it, and then we should be ready."

"Will it hurt the stew to sit there?" she asked me.

"No. As a matter of fact, I may put it back on the stove and let it simmer while we're getting everything else ready." After doing as I'd promised, I sliced the bread into hearty chunks, lathered everything with a bit of butter I'd doctored with some garlic, and then put it all on a sheet under the broiler.

In no time at all, we were ready.

"If you'll set the table, I'll finish up here," I told her.

She popped out of the kitchen and then popped right back in.

"Do I have an insurrection on my hands already?" I asked her.

"It's already been taken care of," she said.

"Are there bowls in front of each place or large plates?" I asked.

Paige's left eyebrow went up. "Oops. I'll be right back."

Two minutes later, she returned. "There are bowls, at least now."

"Thanks," I said, laughing at her expression. I transferred the stew into a large tureen and put the garlic bread onto a sterling silver platter. After placing them both on the serving cart, I said, "Let's go. It's show-time."

"It all looks amazing, but what are we going to do for dessert?" Paige asked me.

"If anyone's still hungry, they can have leftover donuts, because I'm not making anything else."

Paige looked a bit disappointed. "I was hoping for some peach cobbler."

I had to laugh. "Fine. After we eat, I'll whip some up. It's not that hard."

"No. I'm asking too much."

"It's a good thing we're friends, then," I said. "In fact, let me make it right now, and it will be ready by the time we're finished eating our stew."

"What about the hungry crowd out there waiting for dinner?" she asked.

"The longer they wait, the better my stew will taste to them," I told her.

I whipped up a batch of simple peach cobbler, a recipe Momma had taught me when I'd turned ten years old. It used self-rising flour, sugar and milk in equal amounts, some butter, cinnamon, vanilla, and, lucky for me, canned peaches. The oven was mostly preheated from the broiling, so that helped a lot. I set the timer on my phone for forty minutes, and we were finally ready to go.

"What is this?" Bess asked as she looked at her portion of the meal I'd just made.

"It's rustic chicken stew," I told her.

"The word rustic covers a multitude of sins," Frank said.

"Enough," Aunt Jenny said sharply, raising her voice to a bark, something that was out of character for the woman I'd just met. "Suzanne was kind enough to provide our meal, and we will not criticize it, is that understood?"

"Sorry," Frank mumbled under his breath as he took a spoonful. "Hey, that's good. Seriously."

"Thank you. Seriously," I replied.

"It's really tasty," Sandy added. "But I thought Calvin was the chef here, not you. No disrespect intended," she added quickly.

"None taken," I said. "I'm well aware that I'm no match for Calvin in the kitchen."

"So where is he?" Bobbi asked.

"He's handling something else for me at the moment," Aunt Jenny said, making it clear by the tone of her voice that she wasn't discussing it further. "Suzanne, this is wonderful."

"Thanks."

"Wait until you taste dessert," Paige said. "It's Suzanne's famous peach cobbler."

"I don't know about being famous," I amended, not wanting to get their hopes up too much.

"Suzanne, you shouldn't have," Aunt Jenny said.

"What can I say? It was a request I couldn't refuse," I told her with a grin as I pointed to Paige.

"It wasn't that much trouble, honest," she said quickly.

"I was happy to do it. I'm glad to see that you stock vanilla bean ice cream. I wouldn't serve cobbler without it."

"Well, I, for one, am going to save some room for dessert," Aunt Jenny said.

After ten minutes, everyone seemed to be finished. As Paige and I cleared the dishes, I glanced down at Aunt Jenny's bowl. She'd made a real show of enjoying the meal, but it was hard to see if she'd actually eaten any of it.

"Was it all right?" I asked her softly.

"It was amazing. I can't wait to try that cobbler."

As she said it, my phone timer went off, an old-fashioned car horn tone I just loved. "That's my cue," I said as I shut it off.

Paige followed me into the kitchen, and as I pulled the cobbler out, I saw that it had turned out beautifully. "Grab the ice cream, would you?" I asked her.

"I'm on it," she said.

"Aunt Jenny didn't eat much," I said as I put the pan down on hot pads.

"She doesn't these days," Paige said. "I don't press her on it. She's pretty private about it."

"Then I won't, either," I said. I scooped out a small portion of cobbler into a bowl and added a bit of ice cream. "I'll be right back," I said.

I placed it in front of Aunt Jenny and said, "Be careful. It's hot."

"Thank you, Suzanne," she answered. I'd chosen large enough bowls for everyone so they couldn't see how meager Aunt Jenny's portion was. Paige was right behind me, delivering bowl after bowl of cobbler and ice cream to everyone else.

"No, thank you," Bess said. "I'm watching my calories."

"I'm not," Frank said. "I'll take hers too."

"On second thought, it would be rude not to try a bit of it," Bess replied, snagging the bowl before Frank could claim it.

Everyone made the appropriate appreciative noises, and I saw as we cleared the table that Bess had eaten every last bite of her dessert.

Maybe she wasn't all bad after all.

"I'm glad there's a dishwasher," I told Paige as we scraped bowls and stacked them in the essential machine, one I didn't have at Donut Hearts, mostly so I'd have an excuse to keep Emma around. She'd grown into a woman in the years since she'd started working for me, and I knew that she and her mother would proudly carry on the tradition of Donut Hearts long after I was gone.

And I knew in my heart that I was indeed gone.

The donuts I'd made that morning were probably the last ones I'd ever make.

It was as though a switch had been thrown in my head.

I was done.

And not just with donutmaking.

Also with amateur sleuthing.

Let someone else, say, the police, solve any new crimes that happened in my proximity.

I had had enough.

Or so I thought.

Chapter 13

"Suzanne, our hostess wants you two back out in the dining room," Bobbi said as she came into the kitchen.

"What's up?" I asked as I dried my hands on a dishtowel.

"I have no idea, but she said she couldn't get started without you," Bobbi explained.

"I suppose the rest of this can wait," I told Paige. "Let's go see what's going on."

"Thank you for coming back in, ladies," Aunt Jenny said. "Please take your seats," she added rather formally.

Once we'd settled in, our hostess spoke in a strong, clear voice. "I now know, with very little doubt, who stole Suzanne's necklace."

It set everyone off, but Aunt Jenny held up her hands, and everyone quieted instantly. "This is not a question-and-answer session. You are to listen to what I have to say, and then I am retiring to my room for the night."

No one dared make a peep after that.

When Aunt Jenny saw that everyone was going to obey her command, she continued. "If the necklace hasn't been returned to the hallway table by the door at midnight, I will inform the police, who will come and search the premises. No one will leave. No one will move without my permission."

"You can't just keep us here as your prisoners," Frank told her.

"Then leave," she said. I knew she was bluffing, and so did Paige, but the others did not. "Just know that if you choose to leave the property, I will assume that you are guilty, and I will immediately take steps to see that you are punished for your actions. This weekend has been a second chance for most of you, an opportunity to prove yourselves to me one final time. Any who fail to take advantage of that will be cut out completely from any and all monies from me and my estate, including any ongoing payments currently being made. As I said earlier, in addition, all prizes from this weekend will be forfeited and put back into my estate."

The announcements caught all of them by surprise, and I had to wonder if Frank and Bess might not have been feeding at her trough as well as Sandy and Bobbi. "I can't tell you how disappointed I am in the guilty party," Aunt Jenny said, "but there is one small window of redemption available to you, and I urge you to take it. Now, I'll say good night."

With that, she left us, with Roberta just behind her. Her assistant had eaten at the table with the rest of us, and I would make sure there would be plenty of food for Calvin when he returned.

If he returned.

Once Aunt Jenny was gone, there were accusations, sniping, and general insult and insinuation cast among the group.

"Come on, Suzanne. We don't need to listen to this," Paige said.

"Sit back down. We can't afford to miss this," I told her softly as Frank spoke.

"I saw you sneaking around the hallway last night, Sandy, so don't bother denying it."

"I was looking for something to read," Sandy said. "I finished my book early, and I needed something to put myself to sleep. It's like an addiction with me."

"What were *you* doing up in the middle of the night, Frank?" Bobbi asked, surprising everyone.

"I couldn't sleep," he said with a frown. "Is that okay with you?"

"I don't have a problem with it, because I didn't take the necklace," she said, surprising me again with her show of backbone.

"So you think you've got some money coming your way, and now you're bulletproof? She's not giving us anything. I have a feeling that was her plan all along," Frank said.

"That's ludicrous," Paige snapped, letting herself be drawn into the argument.

"I don't think so." Frank studied her for a moment and then added, "I think we should all be looking at you. You had the best opportunity to steal that necklace, and you are the only one who hasn't won anything so far. Getting a bit of your inheritance early, are you?"

Paige came up off her chair, but I held her back, though a part of me had wanted to see what she'd do to Frank. Her face was red as I leaned in. "Don't let him win, Paige. I know you didn't take it, and Aunt Jenny does too. Do any of the rest of them really matter?"

"No, of course not," Paige answered, settling back into her chair.

Sandy ignored what had just happened and turned to Bess. "Can you prove that you didn't take it?"

She hesitated, stared a hole right through her, and then shook her head. "I cannot. Nor do I need to explain anything to you. I didn't steal it."

"So everyone claims," Frank said. "But if it's not returned, we're all going to lose something. Well, everyone but Paige," he added with more than a hint of spite in his voice.

Bess threw up her hands. "This conversation bores me. I'm going to bed early. Good night, all."

"I'm going too," Sandy said as she stood up.

"No reason for me to stay up," Bobbi added.

That left the three of us: Frank, Paige, and me.

"Care to play some cards?" Frank asked us.

"No, I believe we're through here," I told him. "Are you coming, Paige?"

"I wanted to go half an hour ago, remember?" she asked.

"Good night, Frank."

"Yeah. Right. Whatever."

We left him sitting there alone, and I suddenly realized that I'd left a bit of a mess behind for Calvin. There was no way I could live with that. "You go on. I'm going to finish cleaning up," I told Paige.

"I'll help," she volunteered.

"Actually, I wouldn't mind a little time alone to get my thoughts together," I told her. "That's okay with you, isn't it?"

"Not helping you clean up? I can learn to live with that," she said with a light chuckle. "See you soon."

"You can count on it," I said as I disappeared into the kitchen. I hoped Frank didn't join me, because if he did, I would either throw him out or leave myself.

Fortunately, I had the kitchen to myself. He was probably afraid if he came in, I would put him to work.

As I started making things right again, I wondered where Calvin was, how he'd fared, and how soon we'd be rescued from this prison, but most of all, I thought about who might have taken my necklace. Okay, Aunt Jenny's necklace. It helped to think of it that way, as I still hadn't made up my mind if I was going to accept it. It was a bold move, stealing the jewelry from our room and hiding it somewhere no one would be able to find it. Then again, the thief had done a good job, because none of us had a clue where it might be. There was no doubt in my mind that Aunt Jenny meant every word she'd said. Who could blame her? Her kindnesses had been met with mostly scorn and indifference at best. Did she really know who had taken the necklace, or was it a bluff? I already knew that I'd never play poker with the lady.

Even *I* couldn't tell if she'd been telling the truth or not.

Would the thief return the necklace in time, a guilty conscience weighing on them, or would they brazen it out? I supposed that depended on the thief.

Once I had things in order again, I left a note for Calvin.

"Hope you don't mind, but I invaded your kitchen again.

If you get back in time, enjoy the stew and dessert I left for you in the fridge.

See you in the morning.

Suzanne.

"P.S. If you want donuts, you're going to have to make them yourself."

There was nothing else I could do, so I headed off to bed.

Paige was already asleep, but it had been a big day for us all, even though she hadn't been up nearly as early as I'd been.

I fell asleep the moment before my head hit the pillow, but I tossed and turned most of the night, at least until I heard a body falling outside our room, a distinctive thud that left no doubt in my mind that someone had fallen out there, either by accident or by design.

Chapter 14

"Hey. Did you hear that?" I asked Paige softly.

No response.

I turned on my cell phone light to see if Paige was actually sleeping that soundly, but to my surprise, she wasn't in her bed, though it was a rumpled mess.

Had *she* been the one who had fallen?

I rushed out the door. "Paige? Are you okay?"

Still no response.

I flipped on the hall light and saw that there was indeed a body lying on the floor, but it wasn't Paige.

It was our hostess, Aunt Jenny, and from the depth the letter opener was jammed into her chest, I doubted there was anything I or anyone else could do to save her.

Chapter 15

"Aunt Jenny? Can you hear me?" I asked as I leaned over her to see if there was any sign of life left in her.

Our hostess looked at me for an instant, and I could swear she was trying to speak. Lowering my ear to her lips, I said, "Tell me who did this to you."

But there was no response.

Her eyes suddenly glazed over, and her body went limp.

I searched for a pulse that I knew I wouldn't find, but I had to try.

There was nothing there, not even the slightest trace of life left in her.

And that was when I heard Roberta scream. When she got her breath back, Aunt Jenny's assistant stood over me and shouted, "Suzanne, why did you do it? She honestly cared about you."

"I didn't do anything! I heard a noise, I came out into the hallway, and I found her like this," I protested as Roberta pushed me aside and took my place at her employer's side.

Roberta quickly came to the same conclusion that I had.

Aunt Jenny was dead.

But why would someone kill her? That was when I realized it had to be about the necklace. Whether she'd been bluffing or not about knowing who the killer was, they'd obviously taken the threat to heart. But why not just return the blasted thing? I had to wonder, but there wasn't time to speculate as some of the others rushed into the hallway.

Oddly enough, Bess and Frank, both looking disheveled, came out of the same room! What was that all about? I took it all in as Paige appeared with a sandwich.

"What's all the ruckus?" She dropped her plate the moment she saw her aunt lying there and knelt down beside her. "Who did this?"

"I found Suzanne kneeling over her body," Roberta said, the condemnation in her voice dripping freely.

"I was in bed. I heard a noise, you weren't there, so I thought you might have fallen. I checked on what happened and saw Aunt Jenny lying right there. Again, I had nothing to do with it."

"Did you actually *see* her stab Jenny?" Frank asked Roberta.

"No," she admitted. "I thought I heard something too, so I decided to investigate. That's when I found *her*." Roberta turned to me. "I'm sorry. I shouldn't have accused you. It just looked bad."

"I get it," I told her, though Frank and Bess were still looking at me askance. There was still no sign of Bobbi or Sandy. "We need to check on the other two," I added.

"Do you think they're dead too?" Roberta asked in disbelief.

"I just think it's prudent to take a roll call," I told them. Was one of them hiding in their room after committing the murder, or had they fled the scene, not knowing that the bridge was out?

I knocked on both doors, and the women soon appeared from their respective bedrooms, both clearly newly woken or acting the part.

"That just leaves Calvin," Bess said.

"Is he not back yet?" I asked Roberta.

"Back? Where did he go?" Frank demanded. "What are you keeping from us, Suzanne? You clearly know more than we do."

"The storm last night took out the bridge and the cell phone tower," I told them, knowing that it was going to cause a riot, but they deserved to know that we were trapped in this house with a killer and no end in sight.

"What? I don't believe it," Frank snapped. "I'm going for help."

"I'll go with you," Bess said.

"We can all go, but it's not going to do any of us any good," I told them.

"We'll just see about that," Frank said. "And you can all find your own way out of here. Come on, Bess."

She went with them, and Paige asked me, "Should I try to stop them?"

"Why? The bridge will do it for us. Let's cover Aunt Jenny's body with a blanket."

"Can we pull that thing out of her chest first?" Roberta asked, staring at the letter opener's handle. "It's grotesque."

"We don't touch a thing," I ordered. "The police are going to want to see everything just the way we found it."

Paige grabbed a blanket from our room, and we carefully draped it over Aunt Jenny's body. The letter opener tented the fabric up a bit in the middle, making it look more than a bit ridiculous, but my instincts were sound. I wasn't about to disturb evidence that might help catch the killer. I'd just sworn off being an amateur sleuth for the rest of my life, but that was before someone had murdered this dear, sweet lady under my nose.

I was going to figure out who did it if it was the last thing I did.

Frank and Bess returned a few minutes later.

"Back so soon?" Paige asked them sarcastically.

"Ha ha. Very funny," Frank said. "What do we do now?"

"Let's all go into the lounge," I said.

"Why should we listen to you?" Bess asked.

"Because she's solved more murders than anyone you've ever met," Paige snapped in my defense. "We're all going to do exactly as she says. Do you understand?"

"Fine," Frank said, giving in, albeit a bit reluctantly. "Whatever."

"This is a nightmare," Sandy said.

"What happens with the prizes we won? We shouldn't be penalized just because someone killed Jenny," Bess protested.

"You heard her earlier. Unless that necklace is on the hall table, the contests were voided at midnight," I said as I glanced at my phone. It was a quarter after, past her deadline.

We all walked down the hall together, but the necklace wasn't there.

"One of *you* took it, didn't you?" Bobbi asked Frank and Bess.

"What? Of course not," Frank protested. "Why would we do that?"

"Because it was the only prize unaccounted for," Sandy answered. "I wouldn't put it past either one of you to steal it if you thought you could get away with it."

"I resent that," Bess said shrilly.

"Resent all you like," Sandy said, finding some backbone of her own to stand up to the brash rival.

"We didn't take it," Frank said defiantly.

"Maybe you don't have it on you, but one of you could have stashed it in your room since we searched it earlier," Bobbi said.

"Go on. Look again. I don't care."

"That's not a bad idea," I said. "Let's search *all* of the rooms again."

"What's the point?" Bess asked. "We already did that once this evening."

"Yes, and the killer might just think they got away with it," I said. "Come on, we can start in the room Paige and I are sharing. We have nothing to hide."

"Well, I'm not going with you," Bess said.

"As a matter of fact, you are, even if we have to drag you," Paige answered. "From this moment until the police come, no matter when that might be, we are all staying together."

"What if I have to go to the restroom?" Sandy asked.

"Then we all go together. Half of us will stand outside, but nobody, and I mean nobody, is alone from this point forward."

No one pushed back, at least not yet, so I took it as a win. We all stepped delicately around our late hostess's body and entered our room. After a quick but thorough search, nothing was found. I'd been half afraid that someone had planted something in our room to cast suspicion on us, but fortunately, that hadn't happened.

"Where next?" Paige asked me.

"Frank's room," I said. I wanted to see if his bed had been slept in at all since I'd spotted him coming out of Bess's room.

It hadn't been. "You're pretty neat for someone who was supposedly sound asleep," Sandy said.

"So what?" Frank asked. "What business is it of yours?"

"Frank, I saw you come out of Bess's room, so there's no use denying it," I said. There were a few looks of astonishment on the other faces, but I saw that Roberta hadn't been surprised, since she'd been standing in the hallway with me when they'd exited together.

"If you're all finished with your sick and perverted speculation, search the room. You'll see it's clean," Frank barked.

Paige and I took the bathroom while the others crowded in the doorway. I found an inordinate number of washcloths on the floor, along with three used towels, which seemed rather excessive to me. "Wow. How many showers have you taken since we've been here?" Bobbi asked him.

Frank didn't answer. I wondered if something might be hiding in one of the towels, but after I looked through them, they were clean. Not literally, but figuratively, anyway.

Next up was Bobbi's room. It was an uneventful search until I opened the night table drawer by her bed.

"Paige, come here," I said.

She looked where I'd been pointing. "Those two are the mates to the letter opener someone used to kill Aunt Jenny."

"I found two of them a bit ago," Bobbi said, her face red in anger. "So what? I stumbled across them, and I'm kind of compulsive about things like that. I grabbed them both, but one was already missing! You've got to believe me."

"I don't know. It sounds kind of convenient to me," Bess said.

"Would I be stupid enough to keep the other two if I'd used the third one as a murder weapon?" she asked.

"You were in a panic," Frank explained. "You probably weren't planning to kill her, but she accused you of theft and exposure, so you stabbed her. It makes perfect sense to me," Frank said smugly.

"Why was she carrying it around with her in the first place, then?" I asked him. "It doesn't make sense to have one and not the other two."

"Maybe that's what she wants us to think," Bess chimed in.

Sandy took a deep breath. "Bobbi, I don't mean any disrespect, but does *anyone* here really think she's devious enough to plan it that way?"

"I'm not even offended that you just called me stupid," Bobbi answered, though it was clear she was a little peeved by the comment.

"Not stupid, just not devious," Sandy corrected her gently. "There's a difference."

"Maybe what we've seen from her this weekend has *all* been an act," Frank said. "She could have set this up from the start. I know she's been acting this way for the past three weekends Jenny has held these little torture parties, but that doesn't mean she's not clever underneath the surface."

"I'm not, though," Bobbi protested. "Sandy's right. I don't have it in me. Besides, look at my robe sleeves. Do you see any blood on them?"

"The letter opener mostly sealed the wound," I explained to her. "There wouldn't be any blood splatter, especially not that we could see without a microscope. The blade most likely acted as a dam, keeping the blood contained."

"Ew, how could you possibly know that?" Sandy asked.

"This isn't the first knifing victim I've seen," I admitted.

"It was a letter opener, not a knife," Frank reminded me.

I grabbed a tissue and picked up one of the remaining letter openers. "Tell me that doesn't look like a blade to you," I said as I waved it under his nose.

"Put that thing back!" he snapped. "You're the one who said we shouldn't disturb any evidence."

"Thus the tissue," I told him, but he'd been right. In my frustration with the man, I'd broken my own suggestion, which wasn't a particularly good way to lead.

"The letter openers don't prove anything," Bobbi said again.

"Let's keep searching," I said, ignoring her statement. I thought it was at least a possibility Bobbi had found all three letter openers and used one on our hostess. It came from always thinking the worst about someone, and I hoped that someday, I'd be able to break the habit.

There was nothing else in her room, so we moved to Bess's. It was fairly obvious that an assignation had taken place there earlier, but the only other thing we found out of the ordinary was a large wad of paper towels in the wastebasket. "I spilled some of my liquid eyeliner on the counter," she said, and I saw smudges of black ink all over the paper. "It was a real mess."

"You wouldn't think you'd need full makeup to do what you two were clearly doing," Paige said, getting in a dig about them cohabitating for the night.

"You're just jealous," Bess said snidely.

"Of him? You can have him," Paige replied. "I'd rather be alone than pair up with somebody like Frank."

"Hey, I'm standing right here, and for the record, you could do a lot worse. At least I've got an alibi for the time of the murder. Right, Bess?"

"That's right," she answered after a slight pause. "And so do I."

"We'll get into all of that after we search Roberta and Calvin's rooms," I said. I apologized to the assistant. "I'm sorry, but it's only fair."

"It's fine with me," she said. "I don't have anything to hide."

And at least as far as we could tell, she didn't.

Calvin's room hadn't been touched, and I worried about the man's safety for just a moment, but my thoughts were mainly on Aunt Jenny and finding out who did it before help arrived.

"So where does that leave us?" Frank asked.

"We need to go back to the lounge and regroup," I told them.

"Why are we listening to you again?" Bess asked sarcastically.

"Because ignoring me makes you look guilty," I told her flatly, though I didn't believe that was necessarily true. Still, I needed to press them all while I had them nearby. Once the police came, it was very possible many, if not all of them, would lawyer up, so I had a limited amount of time to work with.

"Come on, you heard the lady," Paige said. "Let's go."

A few of them were reluctant to follow us, but in the end, everyone did, including Roberta.

It was time for me to get to work.

Chapter 16

"The cornerstone of any investigation," I explained to the group, "hinges on three legs: motive, means, and opportunity. Let's start with who had the best motive to kill Aunt Jenny."

"It had to be whoever stole the necklace," Bess said scornfully. "You're kidding, right?"

"I'll grant that it's the most probable cause, but it could be a coincidence, though I usually hate them," I said. "Stealing the necklace is the easy guess, and everyone has a motive for that except me."

"You're kidding, right? Suzanne, you're the most likely one of all," Frank said archly.

"What? Why would I steal something that was already mine?"

"Was it, though? Jenny wanted it back, remember? What if you couldn't bring yourself to return it?"

"That's insane," Paige said in my defense.

"Is it?" Bobbi asked. "In a way, it makes perfect sense. No offense, Suzanne, but we're all being accused of theft, so we can't leave you out."

"Say what you will, but I don't believe it for one second," Paige said, backing me up yet again.

"Hang on," I said. "They're right."

"So you're *admitting* that you took it?" Sandy asked, clearly surprised by what she thought of as an admission of guilt.

"No. Take a breath. I'm agreeing that I had a motive of my own to hide the necklace," I allowed. "I didn't steal it, though. You don't know me, but I'm one of the least motivated-by-money people that you'll ever want to meet. I run a donut shop, for goodness sake, and absolutely no one ever said that was a money machine."

"You're selling it, though," Roberta pointed out. "Why would you do that? Do you need the money?"

"No. I mean, I'm not giving the shop away, but I don't have any immediate need for cash, if that's what you're asking."

"That doesn't even matter. Her mother could buy and sell every last one of us," Paige pointed out. "If Suzanne needed money, her mother would provide it without any questions."

"Oh, there would be a few questions," I corrected her, "but yes, she's there for me if I need her."

"So you say," Frank said.

"Hang on a second. When did *I* become the chief suspect?" I asked them.

"You're not, but you're no better than any of the rest of us," Bess answered. "And don't forget, you were found standing over the body."

"Kneeling, actually," I answered.

"Proximity has to be a part of opportunity," Sandy said.

"Any one of us could have had the means," Paige added.

"Some more than others," Frank said as he glanced meaningfully at Bobbi.

"I already told you, one of the letter openers was already gone when I found them," she protested.

"Where were they, exactly?" I asked, more out of curiosity than anything else.

"Right over there in that drawer, in an orange envelope," she said. "It was mixed in with some other correspondence, but when I lifted it up, I felt something shift inside."

"Was the envelope sealed or open when you found it?" I asked her.

"It was sealed. I had to rip it open," she admitted, realizing that the admission made her look guilty.

"Where is the envelope now? Did you take it back to your room?"

"No, I stuffed it back into the drawer after I got the two letter openers out of it," she admitted. "Two, not three."

I walked over to the drawer and took out the envelope in question, being careful to grab a tissue first and use that to hold around the edges of the paper. When I studied it, I saw in an instant that the bottom flap had been carefully opened at one point and taped back up. The top flap was torn open, and no effort had been made at all to repair the damage to the envelope.

"I'm inclined to believe Bobbi," I told the crowd.

"Why? Because you did it yourself?" Bess asked pointedly.

"Let her talk," Paige snapped. "Why do you say that, Suzanne?"

I pointed out my discovery and explained to them what I thought it meant. "Whoever found the letter openers took one. Whether they were planning to commit murder with it or not, I couldn't say. They sealed it back up to hide the fact that they'd taken it and then left the others for Bobbi to find later."

"Are you saying they found it *during* the contest?" Bess asked. "If that was the case, why didn't they turn it in with the rest of their clues?"

"Maybe because they were already a winner," Frank said as he looked at Sandy. "You didn't need it, did you, so you saved it to use on our hostess."

"That's preposterous," Sandy said.

"So you say," Bess responded.

"Let's face it," I said, trying to get control of the group back. "We *all* had the opportunity, and we all had the means. Motive is the pivotal point here."

"To hide stealing the necklace," Bess said. "We've already covered that."

"Or to disguise another crime they didn't want exposed," I said.

"What are you talking about?" Frank asked me.

"I'm not sure, but what if Aunt Jenny's threat to cut everyone off was the reason she was killed? If the murderer didn't steal the necklace, they might have thought by getting rid of Aunt Jenny, they'd keep the money flowing, at least for a little while."

"I doubt that," Paige said. "Once Aunt Jenny made up her mind about anything, that was that."

"So what would happen if one of you tried to talk her out of cutting you out, and she refused? The killer got mad and stabbed her with the letter opener in anger without thinking it through. That would work too."

"So you're saying the theft *wasn't* the cause of the murder?" Roberta asked me.

"No, I'm just saying that there could be something we're not seeing here."

"If you're right," Frank said, "We have a killer *and* a thief on our hands, and they aren't necessarily connected."

"But what if they are?" Bobbi asked.

"What are you talking about?" Frank snapped.

"They both saw you coming out of Bess's room when they found Jenny's body," Bobbi said. "One of you could have taken the necklace and the other killed her for reasons of your own. That could happen."

"I liked it better when you were a browbeaten loser too scared of your own shadow to talk," Frank told her.

"Hey now, let's at least be civil," Sandy said.

"I think we're all way past that, don't you?" Frank asked. "Bess and I were together for the entire night. We can alibi each other."

"Not the *entire* night," Bess said so softly that I almost missed it.

Paige hadn't, though. "What do you mean?"

"Bess," Frank said, his voice suddenly menacing.

"I'm sorry, but I have to tell the truth. Five minutes before you found Jenny's body, Frank slipped out of my room. He had time to stab her and come back."

"You little idiot tramp," Frank said, turning on her. "I went to my room to check my phone again to see if I had cell service yet. You just blew your alibi too."

Bess nodded. "Yes, but I didn't leave my room. You did."

"So you say." Frank sneered.

"Okay," I said. "Let's get this straight. *Nobody* has an alibi for the time of the murder?"

"No one but Calvin," Roberta said.

"Does he really, though? Do we know for sure he's *not* on the property?" Frank asked.

"We've searched the place twice. He's not here," I reminded him.

"He could have hidden from us both times," Bess answered, getting on board with blaming the absent chef. "What if he did it and then took off again? *Nobody* would have any reason to suspect him."

"But Calvin had no motive to kill Aunt Jenny," I said.

"How about your necklace?" Frank asked. "I think your other rationale is just a smokescreen. The theft of the necklace and the threat of exposure were what drove the killer, and nothing else."

"But Calvin wasn't here to hear her threat," I reminded them.

"She could have made it later, when he came back to the house," Frank said.

"That just doesn't make any sense," I said.

"Now who's grasping at straws?" Paige asked as she stared at Frank.

"I'm not saying that he did it. All I'm saying is that we can't rule him out. If he left for help after lunch, why isn't he back? How long does it take to go get help?"

"Considering the hike he had to make to the next house, it could be a while," I said. "That's a pretty steep cliff where the bridge was ruined. It might take him a while to get help scaling that."

"If he actually left," Bess added as she looked around the room.

"I just realized that there's one place we didn't search the second time," Roberta said quietly.

That's when I realized my error. "Aunt Jenny's room. Why would my necklace be there?"

"Because no one thought we'd check her room after she was murdered," Sandy answered. "The thief could have thought it was a safe place to stash it until they could come back and get it later."

"That's crazy, though. I will admit one thing. I must be losing it. Searching Aunt Jenny's room for clues is the first thing I should have suggested. I must be sleep deprived."

"Then by all means, let's go check it out," Paige said.

I didn't want that crowd traipsing through the scene, but what could I say? I was the one who had insisted that we stick together. No, if I was going to find anything, it was going to be with the rest of them.

There was no necklace there, to my relief, or any other clues that might help us, but it gave me an idea. "None of you are going to like this, but I need to search the body."

"What? No. I can't let you do that," Paige protested. "It's not decent."

"We have no choice," I told her. "If there's a clue somewhere on her body, we need to find it. I'm sorry. You don't have to go with us, but it has to be done."

"No, I'll go. But Suzanne, just be respectful, okay?"

"You know that I will," I answered her, and we all returned to the hallway where Aunt Jenny had been slain. I wasn't all that excited about touching the corpse, but I'd done it before, and I needed facts if there were any to be found.

Chances are it would be done in vain, but I had to know.

For Aunt Jenny's sake.

Chapter 17

I'd touched more than my share of bodies in my lifetime, but it never got any easier. That was a good thing, at least in my book. I knelt down beside Aunt Jenny after I removed the blanket we'd put over her, and then I said a silent plea for forgiveness for disturbing her. After that, I pulled on a pair of disposable gloves I'd gotten from the kitchen. There was no way I was leaving any fingerprints or disturbing anything I didn't have to. I tried my best not to focus on the other folks standing nearby, but I did catch Frank's glance for a moment. What I saw there was a bit of distaste mixed with just a hint of respect. It wasn't easy, what I was about to do, but I felt as though it needed to be done.

"Focus on the details," I told myself softly as I checked her hands for anything she might have been holding when she'd been murdered. There was a hint of a black smudge on one finger. What could have caused it? Taking a tissue I'd brought with me, I rubbed it lightly on the smudge.

It didn't come off.

That meant it wasn't some errant piece of dirt but something that had stained her hand. I took several photos with my phone to get every possible angle I could of the smudge in all kinds of different ways. What had caused it? I didn't know, so I put the thought aside as I kept looking.

In one of her robe pockets, I hit pay dirt.

A piece of standard notepaper was folded up in her right pocket. It was on the same side that had the stain on her hand, and I immediately saw why.

Whoever had printed out the note had used a black pen with a bit of a leak, and some of it had gotten onto the paper. Opening the note, I read aloud,

"I admit it. You were right. I took the necklace, but I know something you don't. Meet me in your husband's study at midnight so we can figure out how to handle this."

"Was it signed?" Bobbi asked, clearly hoping for a miracle.

"No, we weren't that lucky," I said. "I read everything that was on it to all to you. Paige, hand me one of those baggies I brought with us." I'd come with some rudimentary supplies, and sandwich bags were in my improvised kit. After putting the note inside, I closed it and set it aside. I'd taken some photos of the writing as well before I sealed the bag, so I'd be able to reference it later without handling the note itself again.

"Is there anything else in her pocket?" Frank asked. It almost felt as though he'd been expecting me to find something I hadn't come across yet.

Interesting.

I finished my search, and as I stood, I said, "No, that was it. Was there something else we should be looking for?" I asked him.

"No. Nothing I can think of. I was just wondering," he said.

"Okay, then," I allowed.

"What happens now?" Sandy asked me.

"I need to see everyone's hands," I said firmly.

Bess shoved hers into her robe pockets the moment I suggested it, and Sandy started rubbing her hands together, as though the request was causing her some kind of physical discomfort.

"Bess, you first," I said.

"I have a smudge on one hand," she said before she pulled it out of her pocket. "That blasted liner won't come off. It's semi permanent, but I didn't write that note, no matter how it looks."

"Nobody's accusing you of anything," I said.

"Bull. I am," Roberta said defiantly. "You stole the necklace, and you wrote the note."

"Listen, I'm not going to stand here and listen to a *servant* accuse me of anything," Bess said, clearly angry or maybe even feeling guilty about the accusation. "Frank, are you going to let her talk to me like that?"

"She's not saying anything the rest of us aren't thinking," Frank replied calmly.

"You total and utter jerk," Bess said, her voice seething. She tried to slap his face, but he was too quick for her, and he grabbed her wrist before her hand could connect.

"It looks like an ink stain to me," he said as he looked at her hand.

"Go to..." she said and then eased up. "Oh, what's the use? Nobody's going to believe me."

"So, just for the record, are you admitting that you stole the necklace and then stabbed Aunt Jenny when she confronted you about it?" I asked her calmly.

"This isn't some bad TV movie," Bess said. "I'm not confessing to *anything*, especially since I didn't do either thing you're all accusing me of. Are you saying that you aren't going to check anyone else's hands? I noticed Sandy rubbing her hands together so hard it looked as though she was trying to start a fire."

"I rub my hands together when I'm stressed out," Sandy explained, showing that her hands were indeed inflamed. "It's a coping mechanism, but I don't have any ink on them," she added as she held up her hands for all of us to see. "See for yourselves."

"What about Bobbi?" Bess asked.

"They're clean, mostly because I didn't do anything," she said, "which is more than I can say for you."

"Listen, you mouse, I've had about enough of your lip. Do you hear me?"

Bobbi backed down a bit. "Or what?"

"Or I'll make you sorry for daring to open your mouth to me," Bess answered as she took a step toward the woman.

She never made it, though.

Frank grabbed her arm and held her in place.

"If you want to keep that hand, I suggest you remove it, and I mean right now," Bess hissed.

"Fine. Just don't try to distract us by accusing everyone else," he said as he pulled his hand away.

"You are a pig through and through," she told him. "You know that, don't you?"

He just grinned at her and said, "Oink."

"Let's not get off track," I said. "Paige, Roberta, I still need to see your hands."

"Why are you still wearing those gloves, Suzanne?" Roberta asked me pointedly. It was clear that she still suspected me. Given the circumstances in which she'd found me looming over her employer's body, I couldn't even really blame her.

Making a show of it, I pulled off each glove and showed my hands to the group. "There. Satisfied?" I asked.

"Why are they so red?" Bobbi asked.

"They must have gotten hot in the gloves," I allowed.

"I have nothing to hide," Paige said as she showed us her pristine hands, with Roberta quickly following suit.

"It looks like you're the winner," Frank said to Bess. "Should we tie her up until the police come?" he asked with a smile.

"Nobody, and I repeat nobody, is going to tie me up," Bess said.

"That's not how you felt last night," Frank said as he leered at her.

"Oh, shut up, would you?" Bess asked. "Come into my room. There's some liner left in the tube. You'll see."

"What is that going to prove?" Sandy asked her. "You could have used it to cover up the ink stain after you couldn't get it off your hand."

"Do you honestly think I'm that devious?" she asked incredulously.

"That's exactly how devious I think you are," Sandy said, standing her ground.

"Fine, don't believe me," Bess said. A thought suddenly occurred to her. "Frank used an awful lot of black towels and washcloths."

"So what? Hygiene is important to me," the bantam man said.

"What if you used them to scrub your hands to get the ink off of them? The ink wouldn't show up on a black towel, would it?"

"Don't try to pin this on me, lady," he snapped. "You're the only one with ink on her hands."

"I already told you, it's eyeliner," she said angrily. "Having it on my hands should prove that I *didn't* do it."

"How do you see it that way?" I asked her.

"Think about it. If I'd written that note and gotten ink on my hands, do you honestly think I'd be stupid enough to move one inch until all traces of it were gone? I didn't know about the note, so there was no reason for me to try that hard to get my hands clean."

"Or you left it on to allow you to use that as an excuse," Bobbi said.

"I thought I told you I'd had enough of your lip!" Bess sneered at her.

"I have just as much right to speak as anyone else does," Bobbi answered, though it was said with a bit less conviction.

"I say we lock her up and wait for the cops to show," Frank said.

"The police don't even know there was a homicide committed here," I reminded him. "As far as we know, no one even knows that we're stranded if Calvin hasn't made it to help yet," I told the group.

"So does that mean that we're all trapped here with a killer?" Sandy asked, the blood going out of her face.

"That's exactly what it means," Bess replied.

"Then we're not safe," Bobbi said meekly.

"As long as we stick together, we should be fine," I said as I stifled a yawn.

"That's the thing, though," Paige said. She'd been mostly quiet so far unless she'd been defending my honor. "We have to sleep, and I for one don't trust the watch to someone who could be a murderer."

"We can take turns," I said. "We'll go from room to room. Grab a pillow and a blanket. We're all going to spend the rest of the night together in the lounge. There are enough couches for all of us, and we'll keep two people on guard at all times. Unless we have *two* killers on our hands, we should be fine until morning."

"Fine," Frank said. "You sleep first and see how it goes."

"Let's just do what she says," Paige said. "We can work out the details after we're set up out there."

We did as I'd suggested, and soon, four people had couches of their own. Paige looked at me and asked, "Are you really taking the first shift to sleep?"

"It was the only way to get them to agree to my plan," I told her softly.

"Then I'll sleep when you do," she replied.

"No, I need you to watch them while I'm sleeping. You're the only one here I trust, so you've got to watch whoever you're on guard duty with."

"I get that," Paige said as she nodded. "Okay, it's a deal."

"What are you two whispering about over there?" Frank asked. "Planning your next victim? In case you've got any crazy ideas, I demand that you two *don't* watch over us together. I don't trust the two of you any more than I can throw you."

"We have no problem with that," I said, offering a smile I didn't feel. "The first team with watch duty is Paige and Bobbi."

"Why do you get to decide?" Bess asked peevishly.

"You get to sleep first. Stop complaining," Paige snapped at her. The stress of the events was wearing on her, and I felt a little bad about taking a rest break before she could.

"Do you want to nap first?" I offered. "I can stay up."

"No, I'm fine," she said. "Get some rest. What do you think, three-hour shifts for the watch crew?"

I glanced at my phone. "Let's make it two. Wake me and Sandy at two a.m.," I said. "Unless there are any objections?"

No one had any. "Fine. It's a plan. Oh, and if anyone needs to go to the restroom, we do it in threes."

"Who's going to chaperone *me*?" Frank asked. "In case you all didn't notice, I'm the only rooster in this hen party now that Calvin is missing in action."

"Two of us will stand guard outside of the bathroom," I told him. "In fact, let's take those breaks now."

"But I don't need to go right now," Bobbi complained.

"Then don't," Bess snapped. "Let's get this over with. I'm exhausted."

"Fine," I said. "Sandy, you and Paige go with Frank. After he's finished, come back here. The rest of us can use the restroom down the hall. Meet back here when you're finished."

Bobbi, Bess, and I finished up and returned to the lounge, but there was still no sign of the other group.

"What's keeping them?" Bess complained. "I want to go to bed."

"Not without them," I said. "Come on, let's go see what's going on."

We walked down the hallway together to the other bathroom, and as we turned the corner, I saw Paige lying on the floor in a heap, a vase shattered beside her.

Apparently, we'd flushed out the killer, but not before she—or he—had been able to strike again.

Chapter 18

"Paige?" I cried out as I knelt down beside her to check for a pulse. I couldn't lose my friend! It was unthinkable.

"What? Suzanne? What happened?" Paige asked as she stirred awake.

"Somebody clobbered you with a vase," I said as I looked around. "Where are Sandy and Frank?"

"I don't know," she said.

That was when we heard someone pounding on the door from inside the bathroom. "Let me out of here," Frank yelled. I noticed that something had been shoved under the door, effectively locking it in place.

Grabbing a slim book from the table nearby, I was able to knock the wedge out and free the door. "Very funny," Frank said when he noticed Paige struggling to sit up. "What happened?"

"Sandy must have hit Paige when her back was turned," I said, feeling remorseful since I'd been the one who'd selected the teams. That blow could have just as easily killed Paige as stunned her, and I was responsible. *Nonsense*, I told myself quickly. I hadn't swung that vase, intent on killing again; Sandy had, and it was pretty clear that she was our killer, and most likely our thief as well.

"She couldn't have gotten far," I said. "Let's go find her."

As we started searching, Bobbi asked, "What set her off? She could have waited until the police came and gotten away with it."

As Paige rubbed her head, she admitted, "I'm afraid that was probably my fault."

"How is that even possible?" I asked her.

"While we were waiting on Frank, I mentioned that I'd read in a recent mystery novel that the police could find microscopic particles of ink on someone's hand regardless of how much they scrubbed, so the killer wasn't being as clever as they thought they were. How stupid was I to tell the murderer I knew they would be caught!"

"You had no way of knowing," I said, trying to console her as best I could.

"Come on. I had a one-in-five shot of telling the wrong person."

"One in six," Roberta corrected her.

"Suzanne didn't kill Aunt Jenny. I'd stake my life on it."

"And yet you had no problem believing that I could do it," Bess said.

"No problem at all," Paige replied, staring her down, almost daring her to say something else.

"What do we do when we find her?" Frank asked. "It could take the police days to get here. It's going to be hard to hold her until then."

"We have to do the best we can," I said, "but let's not borrow trouble. We need to find her before she comes up with any more weapons. She's already killed once. I've got a feeling if she thinks she can get away with it, Sandy will try to kill the rest of us without any compunctions if it means she gets away with murder."

"And a necklace worth a hundred grand," Bess added.

"If she's the one who stole it," Bobbi replied.

"She took it," Bess said with more conviction than she had any right to feel.

"We'll ask her once we've captured her," I said. "In the meantime, I couldn't care less about the missing necklace. All I want is to find the woman who murdered Aunt Jenny."

"I'll second that," Paige said. "Let's go."

"Are you sure you're okay?" I asked her.

"I'm fine."

"Really?" I asked her.

"Of course not. I got hit on the head, but I'm not letting that stop me. Come on. What are we waiting for?"

"We're not going anywhere until we arm ourselves first," Frank said. "Sandy has already proved that she's dangerous."

"With a letter opener and a vase?" Bess snorted.

"They might not be conventional weapons, but they worked just fine, didn't they?" Frank replied.

For once, Bess didn't have an answer for that.

"Let's go back into the lounge," I said. "There are fireplace tools there that should serve us all nicely."

We rushed back to the room we'd set up as our temporary camping spot, keeping an eye out for Sandy as we hurried back.

There was a fireplace poker, a set of tongs, and a shovel, all capable of dealing out blows. That took care of half of us.

"What about the rest of us?" Paige asked as Bess, Roberta, and Frank took the cast iron tools.

"I don't know. Look around for something heavy you can swing," I said.

"I'm grabbing this log," Paige said, "at least until I can find something else."

I turned to Roberta. "You've been here a lot more than we have. Do you have any ideas what we can use for weapons?"

"Let's see. There's a croquet set in the shed out back. That's got mallets in it."

"It's too far. How about the kitchen?" I suggested, not wanting to go outside unless and until we had to. "There are lots of things there we can use as weapons."

"Lead on," Paige answered.

In the end, Paige and Bobbi decided on large kitchen knives while I grabbed a heavy maple rolling pin. I wasn't sure I could bring myself to stab someone unless they were threatening me or someone else I loved, but I'd have less compunction about clobbering them with a heavy wooden pin. After all, I'd done it before. It seemed as though things were coming full circle for me. During an early confrontation with a killer, I'd used a rolling pin as a weapon, and here I was using one again.

Hopefully, for the very last time.

Once we were all armed, I nodded to the group. "No matter what we think of each other right now, we're on the same mission. We need to find Sandy and subdue her before she can strike again. And I mean by any means necessary. Are we agreed on that?"

There were a few nods, but I noticed that Bobbi hadn't responded. "You don't have to attack her if you can't bring yourself to do it, but you still have to come with us."

"I know," she said, her voice almost a whimper.

"Bobbi," Bess said, facing off with her. I prepared myself to step in, but Bess surprised me. "Listen to me. I've never been a fan of yours, and I know you feel the same way about me, but you've shown a lot of spunk tonight facing me down. Keep that fire in you for Sandy. She's our real enemy here. Okay?"

"Okay," Bobbi said, somewhat buoyed by the other woman's pep talk. "Let's do this."

And then, armed with a ragtag collection of weapons, we started off in search of a killer, hoping to stop her once and for all before she could strike again.

Chapter 19

"**S**hould we split up now?" Frank asked. "If we go in threes, we can cover a lot more ground."

"That sounds good to me too," Bess said. "We're going to end up getting in each other's way with six of us."

"Sandy also has a better chance of picking one of us off," I told them. "I can't make you do anything, but if we all want to be alive this time tomorrow, I believe sticking together is our best course of action."

"I'm with you," Paige said, getting my back immediately.

"Me too," Roberta added.

Bobbi looked at Frank and Bess and then at me. "I'm sticking with Suzanne. She makes the most sense. After all, there's safety in numbers."

"Fine, we'll do it your way," Frank agreed, though it was clear he wasn't all that happy about it.

As we entered the ballroom, I took the lead, trying to grow eyes in the back of my head so I could see Sandy if she was lurking anywhere in the room.

Paige was behind me then Roberta, Frank, Bess, and finally, Bobbi.

I was about to ask Paige to switch places with Bobbi, so when I turned back to speak with her, I saw Sandy try to slip out behind us! Where had she been hiding? That's when I saw there was a jog in the wall that I'd missed. Evidently, everyone else had too.

"Bobbi, look out! She's behind you," I shouted as the browbeaten woman pivoted around, slashing out with her knife without seeing her target.

The blade stuck in Sandy's shoulder, and when the murderer pivoted in pain, she ripped the hilt out of Bobbi's hand, taking the knife with her like some kind of talisman as she fled.

Sandy screamed as she ran away from the group, slamming the door behind her.

"I stabbed her," Bobbi said, staring at the blood on her hand. "I actually stabbed her," she repeated. It appeared to me that the woman was in shock.

"Bess, stay here and take care of her," I said as Paige, Roberta, Frank, and I hurried after Sandy.

She'd been dangerous before, but now that she was wounded, I had a feeling that she was going to be twice as unpredictable.

"There she is," Paige shouted as the door outside closed.

"Is there a flashlight anywhere?" I asked Roberta.

"In the study," she said, "and maybe one in the kitchen too, but that's Calvin's domain, so I don't know where it might be."

"We don't have time for that," I said. I didn't want Sandy finding a place to ambush us again, so we needed to follow her at that moment.

As I raced ahead, I saw that at least there was a full moon, which was something, but I found myself wishing for more light so we could follow her blood trail, which I suspected Sandy was leaving behind with every step she took. Bobbi had stabbed her in the shoulder, but I hadn't been able to tell how deep the cut had gone, just that the blade had stuck in the meat of her body.

"Why don't we just wait for the cops to show up and arrest her if she doesn't bleed out first?" Frank asked me as the group hurried up beside me. We were spread out side by side now to be sure we didn't miss anything.

"She could easily circle around and come back into the house," I told him. "Did you see the look in her eyes when Bobbi stabbed her? Sandy is clearly not in her right mind."

"I still don't get why she'd kill Aunt Jenny," Paige said. "Could this all really be because of a silly necklace?"

"It wasn't silly to her," Roberta said. "I wrote the checks every month to Sandy and Bobbi. Jenny was covering both their expenses, but I found out that Sandy had gotten herself so far into debt that Jenny refused to bail her out again. This weekend was to be her last chance to get any financial aid whatsoever. Jenny didn't hold out much hope that Sandy would turn it all around no matter how much she won, though."

"They could have both just gotten jobs and paid their own way," Frank said.

"That was Jenny's point as well," Roberta answered. "The irony of it all is that if Sandy had just waited a few weeks, she wouldn't have had to do anything."

"What are you talking about?" Paige asked Roberta.

"You weren't supposed to know this, but your aunt's cancer was terminal. She was in a great deal of pain, and her doctors told her she had weeks, if not days, left. I'm sorry that I'm the one to tell you."

"I am too," Paige replied. "I wish Aunt Jenny had said something to me personally."

"She wanted to," Roberta answered, "but she didn't want to burden you with it."

"Folks, I hate to say this, but we need to keep moving," I said gently. "I don't trust Sandy one bit."

"Neither do I," Paige said, her voice filled with icy determination. "She robbed Aunt Jenny of the few days she had left, and now she's going to pay for it."

Without waiting for me, Paige hurried ahead. All the rest of us could do was try to keep up. My friend was on a mission, and Sandy was going to regret what she'd done if Paige had anything to say about it.

I caught up with Paige as we neared the destroyed bridge.

That was when I saw movement in the shadows.

Sandy had found a few trees to hide among, and in a burst of insane strength and speed, she lashed out with the knife Bobbi had used on her, directing it at Paige's heart.

I didn't have to time to warn my friend or to counterattack Sandy myself.

There was only one thing I could do, and I did it without hesitation.

I put myself between the blade and my friend.

Sandy's weapon struck home, but not in her intended target.

She'd stabbed me instead.

Chapter 20

I was hurt, but I wasn't so wounded that I couldn't fight back.

At least not yet.

I knew that I couldn't let Sandy get another shot at me with that knife. Despite the searing pain in my left arm, I used my right arm to grab her close to me so she couldn't lunge at me again. The rolling pin I'd been carrying as a weapon had fallen out of my hand the moment Sandy stabbed me.

So much for being armed.

As I held Sandy close to me, she started cursing me, pushing backward, fighting to get out of my grip so she could lunge at me again with the knife still in her hand.

I had the best hold on her with one good arm that I could get, but her struggles were fueled by her insanity.

In the next instant, I felt Sandy's momentum go backwards, pulling me with her over the edge of the precipice.

It felt as though this was the end for me, but I didn't regret saving my friend for an instant.

It was as noble a way to die as any.

And then I felt someone grab my ankle.

I nearly pulled me *and* my hero over the cliff face, but whoever had me in their grip was strong, and it stopped my fall. As I hit my wounded arm against the cliff side, another shot of pain raced through me, but I wasn't about to complain.

I looked up and saw Paige holding me tight.

"I've got you," Paige said, even as I felt us both starting to slip down into the chasm below.

Then Frank shouted from above me, "Hang on, you two."

It had taken Frank *and* Roberta to keep Paige and me from plummeting over the cliff, but Sandy hadn't been so lucky.

As they pulled me up, I looked down and saw Sandy's lifeless body lying below us. From the angle of her neck on the rocks she'd landed on, she must have died on impact.

Aunt Jenny's murder was avenged, but it wouldn't bring the sweet older woman back. Sandy had robbed us of her presence, and for that, she'd paid the ultimate price.

I hadn't let her go. It had been her own attempt to free herself that had been her downfall. The woman had been so intent on finishing me that she had forgotten everything else, including her location on the edge of a precipice.

Paige pulled off her top and pushed it down onto my knife wound, applying pressure to slow the bleeding. "Good thing you had a sports bra under that," I told her, trying to smile despite the pain.

"I couldn't care less who I flashed right now," she said. "You saved my life, Suzanne."

"And then you saved mine, so we're even," I told her. "What's that noise?" I asked as I heard rotors above us getting closer and closer.

"It must be an inspection crew checking the power lines or the cell phone tower," she said.

"At night? I don't think so," I answered.

The helicopter got closer and closer, and then the pilot set it down in a clearing a hundred feet from us.

Calvin got out and rushed toward us. "We saw a little of what happened. Who is that?" he asked.

"Sandy," Roberta reported. "She killed Jenny."

"What? Jen's dead?" Calvin asked, clearly stunned by the news. "Why would she do that?"

"To cover up her theft," Paige said. "We can explain later. Right now, Suzanne needs to get to the hospital. Can that thing hold all of us?"

"It can take two other people," Calvin said. "I got one of Jenny's friends to loan it to me so I could get her out. I was too late, though."

Roberta surprised me by putting a hand on Calvin's shoulder. "You did the very best you could."

"Maybe, but it clearly wasn't good enough," he answered, choking back the tears.

"Suzanne needs help," Paige insisted.

"Of course," he answered. "Come on," Calvin said as he helped me stand. The pain throbbed even worse once I was erect. "Paige, you're coming with her."

She didn't even argue, since I knew she'd insist on it if Calvin hadn't suggested it. "We'll be back for the rest of you soon," he told Roberta.

She nodded. "No hurry. Take care of her. It's what Jenny would have wanted."

Calvin nodded, and then he helped me into the helicopter.

The last thing I saw as we pulled away was Sandy's broken body lying below us. Her greed had been her downfall, but she'd taken someone special with her. Aunt Jenny hadn't had a lot of time left, but she had deserved to have every moment allotted her, not robbed of it by someone who had cared about money and only money.

Chapter 21

The doctor came in to check on me after he'd treated my stab wound. "How are you feeling now?"

"Still a bit nauseous from the food poisoning I got last week, but the arm's okay at the moment."

"That's because we gave you some painkillers," he said. "Let me guess. You get sick in the morning, and by noon, it's gone."

"Yeah, that's it. How did you know?"

"We ran some blood tests earlier when they brought you in. It's not the best way to find out, but it's good news nonetheless. Ms. Hart, you're pregnant."

Chapter 22

"What? Pregnant? Are you sure?"

"I'm positive," he said. "Is there a Mr. Hart, by any chance?"

"His name's Bishop," I said. "We're married, but I kept my name for my business. Did any of what happened hurt the baby?" I asked.

"No, you're both going to be fine," he said with a smile. "I'd check in with your regular doctor when you get home. He'll need to take out your stitches, and he'll be able to go over your prenatal care then."

"Thanks," I said, stunned by the news. Jake and I had talked about having kids, even trying once or twice, but it hadn't worked out for us.

Until now.

If there had been any doubt in my mind that I was going to change my ways, it was now gone. After all, now, I had more than my own needs and my husband's to consider.

Speak of the devil, and he appears.

Jake came into the room, and he must have noticed the shocked expression still on my face.

"Are you Mr. Bishop?" the doctor asked.

"I am," Jake answered, not taking his eyes off of me. "Suzanne, are you okay? They told me it wasn't bad, but you look as though you've seen a ghost."

"I'll leave you two to it," the doctor said as he shook Jake's hand. "I'll make certain you're not disturbed."

"Thank you. For everything," I told him as he was leaving.

"It was my pleasure. Both times."

"What did he mean by that?" Jake asked, clearly perplexed by the exchange.

"Jake, this isn't the best way to tell you, but it's how I found out, so now it's your turn. We're going to have a baby. I'm pregnant."

I watched his expression, hoping to see joy there. He had lost a child with his first wife from a car wreck, and I wasn't entirely sure how he would react upon learning that he was going to be father again.

There had been no reason for me to worry.

His face broke out into the biggest grin I'd ever seen in my life. "I'm going to be a dad again? That's amazing. Suzanne, you're the best. Nice job."

Nice job? He really was in shock. "Thanks, but I had some help, remember?"

"I need to go get some cigars to hand out," Jake said as he started for the door.

"That can wait awhile," I reminded him. "You traditionally don't hand those out until the baby's born."

"Oh. That's right." He knelt down to kiss me, being careful not to touch my bandaged arm. "Suzanne, this is the best news I've ever had in my life."

"Mine too," I told him. "Before you ask, I've decided to sell Donut Hearts to Emma and Sharon, and as of now, I've investigated my last murder."

"Because of the baby?" he asked.

"No, I'd already decided on both courses of action before I found out," I told him. "It's time. The smell of food in the morning makes me nauseous, which isn't ideal for a donutmaker, but I was ready anyway. I'll make donuts for you at home, but I'm retiring from the profession."

"And from sleuthing?" he asked me.

"I've taken my last chance," I said. "My heart's just not in it anymore. Let someone else handle that. You, for example."

"Sorry, but I'm not going to be able to do that," he said with a grin.

"You're leaving April Springs high and dry?" I asked.

"Nope. I don't have to. Stephen's back on the job tomorrow morning."

I couldn't wrap my head around that. "He left Grace?"

"She's back here with him," Jake said. "In fact, she's waiting outside. She asked me if she could spend some time alone with you, but you'd better do it now before Dot gets here. *Nobody's* going to keep your mother out of here, not even armed guards."

"I know you're not supposed to say anything during the first trimester, but can I at least tell her?" I asked him.

"I'd be disappointed in you if you didn't," Jake said with a broad grin.

Grace came into the hospital room, brushed past Jake without a word, and grabbed my good hand in hers.

"I'm pregnant," we both said at the same time, and then we started laughing.

"It wasn't food poisoning after all," she finally said after we settled down. "When I found out, I told my boss, who suddenly had no problem with me going back to my old territory. There was no way I was going to raise this kid anywhere but April Springs, especially not now."

"I can't believe we're going to have our babies together," I told her.

"Believe it," Grace said with a grin.

"You're glowing. You know that, right?" I told her.

"So are you. Hey, nothing says we can't be pregnant and still look good."

"If you say so, but in six or seven months, we're both going to be as big as houses."

"And what a glorious time we'll have getting there," she answered as Momma rushed in.

She started to say something, and then she studied our faces for a moment. "I don't believe it."

"What, that Grace came back? It's wonderful, isn't it?"

"You're pregnant," Momma said matter-of-factly.

"Jake told you?" I asked.

"He didn't have to. I can see it in your eyes." She glanced at Grace and shook her head. "Then again, maybe I'm wrong. You look pregnant to me too."

"You're two for two, Momma," I told her, and none of us could stop celebrating until a nurse came in and asked us to hold it down.

Chapter 23

I had just finished signing the last document transferring ownership of Donut Hearts to Emma and Sharon when Paige rushed into the lawyer's office.

"Suzanne, you didn't sign anything yet, did you?" Paige asked me.

"I just did," I said. "Meet the new owners of Donut Hearts."

"I hope you didn't do it for the money," Paige told me, a worried look on her face. "This is all my fault."

"I don't know what you're talking about, but I feel good about what's happening here. I hate to break it to you, but as much as I love you, you weren't even a factor in my decision."

"Okay. Congratulations, then?" she asked.

"Thank you," I said as I handed the keys over to Emma and Sharon.

"Don't worry, we'll take good care of the place," Emma said. "You'll see. We'll be good neighbors."

"I'm sure you will," Paige said. "Suzanne, may I have a moment?"

"Of course. We've got to get back to the donut shop," Sharon said.

"Paige, one second." I then turned to the new owners and said, "Don't worry one bit about changing the store's name. You've got my blessing to call it whatever you want to."

"Are you crazy? It wouldn't be the same if it weren't called Donut Hearts," Emma said.

"You really don't have to do that for me," I told them.

"Why do you think we had the name included in the sale?" Sharon asked. "It's Donut Hearts, now and forever, at least as long as we're still running it."

"And that will be a very long time," Emma said. "Come on, Mom. We have work to do."

"Enjoy it," I told them, and as they left, I could hear the happiness in their voices. It had been the right thing to do, and I was glad that I'd done it.

Paige handed me an envelope. "This is for you."

"What is it?" I asked her.

"Open it and see," she said with a grin.

I did as she told me and found a check in it with more zeros than I'd ever seen in my life. "What is this for?"

"It's from the sale of the necklace," Paige said. "Aunt Jenny was right. You got a hundred thousand dollars for it after the commission. I assumed you wouldn't want the necklace after the police got it off from around Sandy's neck."

"She was wearing it when she fell?" I asked.

"Yeah, but her shirt hid it from view. We searched the rooms, but we never searched each other," Paige said with a grin as she tapped the check with one finger. "I hope it's okay that I went ahead and sold it for you."

"You should keep the money," I said, staring at the check again before shoving it back into the envelope.

"No thank you," she said.

"But you didn't get anything," I reminded her.

"That's not quite true," Paige said. "Aunt Jenny left me everything."

"What? Are you serious?"

"Yep. It turns out that I'm rich," she answered.

"So does that mean you're selling the bookstore?"

"Not a chance," Paige said. "I enjoy it too much. I won't have to worry so much about the bottom line anymore, though. That will be nice."

"I would think so," I answered, trying to grasp the fact that my friend was now a multimillionaire.

"Oh, and I'm making good on the prizes Frank, Bess, and Bobbi won too. Aunt Jenny would have wanted it that way."

"Good for you. What about Roberta and Calvin?"

"She left them each more than any of the prizes were worth, so don't worry about them," Paige said. "Are you still glad you sold the donut shop? I could have told you weeks ago, but I wanted to wait until I could personally hand you a check."

"I'm thrilled," I said. I hadn't told anyone my news since that day in the hospital, but I decided to push my luck one more time.

After all, Paige wasn't the only one with good news to share, and I was dying to tell her mine.

RECIPES

Quick and Easy Donut Holes in a Bag

This is a donut recipe that doesn't require much in the way of supplies. We buy premixed muffin mixes for this recipe. They are great
donuts when you're in a rush and still want to feel as though you've
made something by hand. They have the added bonus of being tasty
too!

Ingredients

1 pouch muffin mix (we like Apple Cinnamon Martha White 7 oz.
size)

1/2 cup whole milk

Peanut oil for frying (the amount depends on your pot or fryer)

Directions

Heat enough peanut oil to 365 degrees F to cover the donut holes
you'll be frying.

Stir the milk into the mix until it is well moistened.

Then, using a small cookie scoop or two spoons, drop bits of dough
into the hot oil.

Allow them to fry for 2 minutes, turning halfway through, or until
the holes are golden brown.

Drain on a rack over paper towels and then dust with powdered
sugar.

Yield: 10–12 donut holes

Suzanne's Peach Cobbler

I love peach cobbler, and the beauty of this recipe is that you don't even have to wait until peaches are in season to make it. For me, canned peaches work just fine. A refined palate can probably tell the difference once the cobbler is baked, but I'm the first to admit that I can't. This recipe can be made with items you most likely already have in your pantry, so it's a surefire winner when you need a quick dessert.

I can only dream about having the pantry Suzanne has access to in the book, but even I have the ingredients to whip this up on short notice.

Vanilla ice cream is amazing on this cobbler while it's still warm, but in a pinch, you can eat it without the topping.

Not that I ever do. As a matter of fact, I don't make any kind of cobbler unless I have a supply of vanilla ice cream on hand, which is, fortunately, rarely a problem.

Enjoy!

INGREDIENTS

¼ cup butter, unsalted

½ cup self-rising flour

½ cup granulated sugar

½ cup milk (2% or whole is best, but I've used 1% with good results)

1 teaspoon cinnamon

1 teaspoon vanilla

1 can (15 oz.) sliced peaches in heavy syrup

2 tablespoons cinnamon sugar blend

Directions

Preheat the oven to 350 degrees F. Melt the butter in the dish you'll be using.

In a medium-sized bowl, mix the flour, sugar, and cinnamon together, stirring well. Add the vanilla into your milk and stir before adding to the dry ingredients.

It will look soupy at this point, but don't worry!

The butter should be melted, so pull out the dish (with a hot pad!) and pour the batter directly into the butter mixture.

Do not stir.

Next, add the peaches and juice to the top of the batter.

Again, do not stir.

Finally, sprinkle the top with cinnamon sugar. This step is optional, but I recommend it.

Bake the cobbler for 45 to 50 minutes, or until the top is golden brown and has pulled away slightly from the sides of the dish.

Let cool a bit then serve while warm, adding the ice cream on top.

Serves 3–4

Aunt Jenny's Favorite Apple Cider Donuts

Like Aunt Jenny, I love apple cider donuts, and I enjoy making them in the fall with freshly squeezed cider. If you use bottled and pasteurized cider, you can make these year round!

To me, they taste like autumn!

Ingredients

1 egg, beaten

2/3 cup brown sugar (light or dark works fine), packed tight

3 tablespoons unsalted butter, melted

1/2 cup apple cider (apple juice can be used in a pinch)

2 1/2 cups all-purpose flour

1/2 teaspoon cinnamon

1/2 teaspoon nutmeg

1 teaspoon baking powder

1/2 teaspoon baking soda

2 dashes salt

1 1/2 to 2 quarts peanut or canola oil for frying (depending on the depth of your pot)

Directions

Heat enough peanut or canola oil to allow the donuts to fry at 365 degrees F.

In a large bowl, beat the egg then add brown sugar, melted butter, and apple cider to the wet mixture.

Set that aside, and in another bowl, sift the flour, cinnamon, nutmeg, baking powder, baking soda, and salt together. Add the dry ingredients to the wet in thirds, mixing thoroughly along the way. You'll probably have to use your hands at the end, which I always do.

Refrigerate the dough for at least 30 minutes after it's all incorporated, then roll it out from anywhere to 1/2 to 1/4 inch thick.

Cut out the donuts and fry them for 3 to 4 minutes, turning halfway through.

Drain on paper towels then add powdered sugar immediately, or wait until they're cool and add icing and sprinkles.

Makes 8–10 donuts and holes

If you enjoy Jessica Beck Mysteries and you would like to be notified when the next book is being released, please visit our website at jessicabeckmysteries.net for valuable information about Jessica's books, and sign up for her new-releases-only mail blast.

Your email address will not be shared, sold, bartered, traded, broadcast, or disclosed in any way. There will be no spam from us, just a friendly reminder when the latest book is being released, and of course, you can drop out at any time.

Other Books by Jessica Beck

The Donut Mysteries
Glazed Murder
Fatally Frosted
Sinister Sprinkles
Evil Éclairs
Tragic Toppings
Killer Crullers
Drop Dead Chocolate
Powdered Peril
Illegally Iced
Deadly Donuts
Assault and Batter
Sweet Suspects
Deep Fried Homicide
Custard Crime
Lemon Larceny
Bad Bites
Old Fashioned Crooks
Dangerous Dough
Troubled Treats
Sugar Coated Sins
Criminal Crumbs
Vanilla Vices
Raspberry Revenge
Fugitive Filling
Devil's Food Defense
Pumpkin Pleas
Floured Felonies
Mixed Malice

Tasty Trials
Baked Books
Cranberry Crimes
Boston Cream Bribes
Cherry Filled Charges
Scary Sweets
Cocoa Crush
Pastry Penalties
Apple Stuffed Alibies
Perjury Proof
Caramel Canvas
Dark Drizzles
Counterfeit Confections
Measured Mayhem
Blended Bribes
Sifted Sentences
Dusted Discoveries
Nasty Knead
Rigged Rising
Donut Despair
Whisked Warnings
Baker's Burden
Battered Bluff
The Hole Truth
Donut Disturb
Wicked Wedding Donuts
Donut Hearts Homicide
Sticky Steal
Jelly Filled Justice
The Last Donut
The Classic Diner Mysteries
A Chili Death

A Deadly Beef
A Killer Cake
A Baked Ham
A Bad Egg
A Real Pickle
A Burned Biscuit
The Ghost Cat Cozy Mysteries
Ghost Cat: Midnight Paws
Ghost Cat 2: Bid for Midnight
The Cast Iron Cooking Mysteries
Cast Iron Will
Cast Iron Conviction
Cast Iron Alibi
Cast Iron Motive
Cast Iron Suspicion
Nonfiction
The Donut Mysteries Cookbook

Made in the USA
Middletown, DE
28 November 2023

43869416R00097